P9-DDZ-908

A Treasury of

AFRICAN AMERICAN

CHRISTMAS STORIES

A Treasury of AFRICAN AMERICAN CHRISTMAS STORIES

Compiled
and Edited *by*

Bettye Collier-Thomas

Beacon Press
Boston

Beacon Press
Boston, Massachusetts
www.beacon.org

Beacon Press books
are published under the auspices of
the Unitarian Universalist Association of Congregations.

© 2018 by Bettye Collier-Thomas
All rights reserved
Printed in the United States of America

21 20 19 18   8 7 6 5 4 3 2 1

This book is printed on acid-free paper that meets the uncoated
paper ANSI/NISO specifications for permanence as revised in 1992.

Text design and composition by Michael Starkman at
Wilsted & Taylor Publishing Services

Library of Congress Cataloging-in-Publication Data
Names: Collier-Thomas, Bettye, editor.
Title: A treasury of African American Christmas stories / compiled and edited
    by Bettye Collier-Thomas.
Description: Boston : Beacon Press, [2018]
Identifiers: LCCN 2018017993 (print) | LCCN 2018021638 (ebook) | ISBN
    9780807027936 (ebook) | ISBN 9780807027837 (hardback : acid-free paper)
Subjects: LCSH: Christmas—Literary collections. | American
    literature—African American authors. | African Americans—Literary
    collections. | BISAC: FICTION / African American / Christian. | FICTION /
    African American / Historical.
Classification: LCC PS509.C56 (ebook) | LCC PS509.C56 T73 2018 (print) | DDC
    810.8/033408996073—dc23
LC record available at https://lccn.loc.gov/2018017993

CONTENTS

Note to Readers ix

Introduction xi

The Sermon in the Cradle 1
W. E. B. Du Bois

♦

A Carol of Color 5
Mary Jenness

♦

The Christmas Reunion Down at Martinsville 7
Augustus M. Hodges

♦

The Children's Christmas 14
Alice Moore Dunbar

♦

Christmas Eve Story 20
Fanny Jackson Coppin

♦

Mollie's Best Christmas Gift 26
Mary E. Lee

A Christmas Story 30
Carrie Jane Thomas

◆

Fannie May's Christmas 35
Katherine Davis Tillman

◆

Elsie's Christmas 46
Salem Tutt Whitney

◆

General Washington: A Christmas Story 58
Pauline Elizabeth Hopkins

◆

The Autobiography of a Dollar Bill 76
Lelia Plummer

◆

Mirama's Christmas Test 83
Timothy Thomas Fortune

◆

A Christmas Party That Prevented a Split in the Church 92
Margaret Black

◆

Three Men and a Woman 115
Augustus M. Hodges

◆

It Came to Pass: A Christmas Story 169
Bruce L. Reynolds

A Christmas Journey 175
Louis Lorenzo Redding

♦

Uncle U.S. Santa Claus 186
James Conway Jackson

♦

The Devil Spends Christmas Eve in Dixie 189
Andrew Dobson

♦

One Christmas Eve 192
Langston Hughes

♦

Santa Claus Is a White Man 201
John Henrik Clarke

♦

Merry Christmas Eve 212
Adele Hamlin

♦

White Christmas 217
Valena Minor Williams

Sources 227

NOTE TO READERS

In order to maintain authenticity, as well as the flavor of the period, I have retained the original spelling, punctuation, paragraphing, and chapter and section divisions, except in cases of obvious typographical errors or where the meaning of the text was obscured. Nineteenth-century grammar, idioms, and punctuation deviate from those of today; writers sometimes used semi-colons instead of commas, idiosyncratic capitalizations, and variations in spelling. In a few cases, letters have been added to complete the spelling of a word or a word has been inserted to ensure that a sentence is comprehensible. Several of the stories include dashes in place of the names of towns, cities, and institutions. Authors such as Pauline E. Hopkins and Augustus M. Hodges make the point that their stories are true and that the name of the place or specific institution is omitted to protect the identity of the participants. There are a few silent punctuation changes.

INTRODUCTION

A Treasury of African American Christmas Stories is a collection of little-known short stories and narrative poems written by black writers, journalists, and political activists. These writings, originally published in African American newspapers, periodicals, and journals between 1880 and 1953, are part of the black literary tradition that flourished after the Civil War. This book includes eighteen Christmas stories and four Christmas poems. Six of the writings were published in the late nineteenth century. Fourteen were produced in the period from 1900 to 1939, and two between 1940 and 1953. More than one-third of the writings are from the 1920s and 1930s "New Negro" Harlem Movement, which found expression in what is popularly known as the Harlem Renaissance. The majority of the stories published in the last two decades of the nineteenth century are concerned with correcting the historical record as regards black life and history, and in instructing the black community and others about the political and social issues of the time.

One might ask, What is the nature and function of black literature, especially African American Christmas stories? Why did black political and social activists write Christmas poems and stories? In *The Book of American Negro Poetry*, published in 1922, James Weldon Johnson asserted that black people must create literature because it is a basic aspect of their struggle for equal rights and justice, and it serves as evidence of the African American's intellectual potential.

Journalists, intellectuals, and various activists perceived Christmas as a perfect time to capture the attention of black readers. First celebrated by enslaved Africans, the holiday has evolved through generations who envisioned the birth of Christ as a new beginning and embraced Christianity as a means of survival. Following the Civil War, the holiday became a time for reunion with family and friends and a time for reflection on the successes and failures of families, black communities, and the race as a whole. It was a time for renewing relationships and sharing family stories. It was a time for giving thanks to God for their very existence.

Generations of African Americans have been entertained and dazzled by a stunning array of Christmas poems and stories written by, about, and primarily for black readers. Displaying amazing wit and humor, disclosing the innermost secrets of the black psyche, and probing the depths of African American life and thought, writers of all ages and of different persuasions used the Christmas theme to raise questions about the real meaning of the holiday. Some extolled the virtues of Christianity and stressed the importance of family and community, while others questioned America's commitment to its black citizens. Many of the writers included in this anthology politicized the Christmas theme as a way of bringing attention to the plight of African Americans.

First introduced into American popular culture in the late eighteenth century as St. Nicholas, the mythical figure was popularized in the early nineteenth century as Santa Claus by a member of the New York Historical Society who distributed woodcuts featuring images of a portly white man filling stockings with toys and fruit over a fireplace. The figure grew in prominence as noted writers further embellished his image and wrote stories of his escapades. As giving gifts became a central part of the Christmas celebration, especially for children, stores promoted shopping during the holiday. By the 1850s, newspapers fashioned special sections for holiday advertisements that often featured images of Santa Claus, and stores displayed life-size Santa Claus models and introduced live Santa Clauses. Black and white children alike were mesmerized by stories of Santa Claus and his reindeer flying through the air and delivering gifts to them. The figure was used by parents to persuade their children to be on their best behavior.

During a time when African Americans were being lynched and denied their citizenship rights, it was problematic to have their children worshipping a white Santa Claus. But by the 1880s, it was no longer possible to simply ignore the ubiquitous and benevolent figure of Santa Claus, who invaded the streets of towns and cities, soliciting donations for the Salvation Army to pay for free Christmas meals for families in need. Early African American journalists and political activists intervened to present Christmas and Santa Claus as a way of exploring black cultural traditions and promoting love and hope.

I continue to be amazed at the profundity of the stories, poems, comics, and satirical sketches African American writers produced using the Christmas theme. Straddling the nineteenth and twentieth centuries, this is the first anthology of African American Christmas stories to focus exclusively on stories and poems. This is the third volume of African American Christmas stories that I have compiled and edited. Each volume has been unique in terms of the themes, the writers, and the time period covered. The first publications comprised stories published between 1880 and 1940. This book, as a compilation of the best stories included in the first two volumes, plus five additional stories and narrative poems, includes writings from the earliest period to 1953. All of these Christmas stories were originally serialized in black-owned newspapers and periodicals such as the *Christian Recorder, Indianapolis Freeman, Colored American Magazine, Baltimore Afro-American, Chicago Defender, Washington Bee, Crisis*, and *Opportunity*—essential venues for the majority of nineteenth- and early twentieth-century writers who were excluded from the white press. White publishers were more interested in black caricature than in addressing issues of economic, political, and social oppression of African Americans.

In the late nineteenth and early twentieth centuries, writers such as Lelia Plummer, Augustus Hodges, and T. Thomas Fortune explored themes regarding the impact of slavery and freedom on the lives of black men and women in the North and South. For example, in "The Autobiography of a Dollar Bill," Plummer utilizes the dollar bill as a metaphor for the enslaved African to examine human commodification in slavery. Fortune conveys critical concerns about definitions of black manhood and womanhood, and black male-female relationships in "Mirama's Christmas Test." Augustus Hodges displays unique insight into the multiple issues that engaged black and white Americans in the 1890s, including lynching, interracial relationships, and self-determination. In "Three Men and a Woman," he uses historical fiction to explore the most critical issues of the time. Likewise in "The Christmas Reunion Down at Martinsville," Hodges emphasizes the strength of the black family in slavery and freedom.

As a result of the Great Migration, the black population in New York City, in particular in Harlem, soared. By 1920, Harlem was recognized as a major center for black culture. It was there that the "New Negro Movement," which became known as the Harlem Renaissance, began. African Americans, in celebrating their blackness and African heritage, became more vocal in challenging the notion and image of a white Christ. W. E. B. Du Bois, the editor of the *Crisis*, wrote "The Sermon in the Cradle," in which he declares that Jesus is black! Well-known journalists such as Andrew Dobson used the Christmas theme to raise questions about the relationship of American values to existing patterns of segregation, discrimination, and lynching. For example, in "The Devil Spends Christmas Eve in Dixie," Dobson speaks about trees "loaded with humans." This exquisite and haunting narrative poem was published six years before Billie Holiday popularized "Strange Fruit," a song about the Southern practice of lynching.

Pauline Hopkins, Adele Hamlin, and Valena Minor Williams demonstrate the evolution of African American Christmas narratives that reveal the broad and richly textured context of black life and history in the United States from 1900 to the 1950s, and also illustrate the impact of racial discrimination on the black family. Beginning with Hopkins's "General Washington: A Christmas Story" and ending with Williams's "White Christmas," readers are afforded an opportunity to travel through time and become immersed in the essence of African American culture at the core.

The mythical image of Santa Claus permeates many of the poems and stories, as African Americans pondered the relevancy of the iconic figure to their lives. "Uncle U.S. Santa Claus," and "Santa Claus Is a White Man" obviously reference Santa Claus; however, there are many more stories that explore the multidimensional Santa Claus theme. Whereas a few stories, such as "Elsie's Christmas," "Fannie May's Christmas," and "A Christmas Story," consider questions regarding the identity and significance of Santa Claus in the lives of children. In the nineteenth century, Carrie Jane Thomas views Santa Claus as a force for good. Langston Hughes and John Henrik Clarke, products of the Harlem Renaissance era, deconstruct traditional Christmas values and themes by stripping away the veneer of the jolly old Santa Claus to expose the racist and anti-Christian views and practices that predominated in the white South during the 1930s and threatened the existence of African Americans. "White Christmas," a 1950s story, signals the growing concern of African Americans with the exclusive portrayal of Santa Claus as white.

Gwendolyn Brooks, the recipient of many honors and awards, and a Pulitzer Prize–winning poet, revealed, in a 1950 interview with the *Baltimore Afro-American*, that like most children she raised serious questions about the identity of Santa Claus, the "magnanimous figure clad in red and white who whirled over roofs with no trouble at all." At Christmas in 1925 or 1926, Brooks recalls finding two sets of beautiful doll clothing under her Christmas tree. She knew that the clothes were made for her dolls, Gertrude and Sally, and told her mother which doll each set was for. "Oh, no," her mother gently corrected her, it was quite the reverse. After an extended disagreement, her mother forgot herself and exclaimed, "I ought to know, because I made those clothes myself." Embarrassed by her outburst, her mother tried to distract her child's attention. However, Brooks privately relished the revelation. For her, that was the best Christmas ever, for "at last she knew who it was that deserved her gratitude." Reminiscing about the event, Brooks asserted "It was pleasant to discover that it was my parents who loved me so much, and not a busy flying fairy."

But the real meaning of Christmas, and its attendant images and practices, including Santa Claus, the legendary power of the kiss under the mistletoe, and the magical aura of the story of the Christ child, is in the happiness these beliefs, traditions, and practices bring both to children and adults, as well as in the values of sharing, caring, and loving that are annually celebrated and emphasized in the holiday's traditional ceremonies and activities. For African Americans, Christmas is also steeped in race memory and heritage. Through this rich body of Christmas literature bequeathed to us, we are reminded once again of the complexity of the African American experience.

Although the plots of these Christmas stories are set in different time periods and explore subjects as diverse as slavery, the Civil War, marriage and family, lynching, and miscegenation, most reinforce traditional values and themes that have defined the meaning of Christmas for time immemorial. For example, Mary E. Lee, in "Mollie's Best Christmas Gift," stresses that Christmas is about the birth of Jesus Christ and his gift to humanity. Bruce L. Reynolds, in "It Came to Pass," and Louis Lorenzo Redding, in "A Christmas Journey," emphasize that Christmas is about loving, sharing, caring, and forgiving.

This rich and complex collection of poems and stories reminds us once again of the enduring significance of the Christmas holiday among African Americans. We are allowed a glimpse into a past that highlights the love, hope, faith, aspirations, holiday traditions, family values, spirituality, and fears common to our ancestors yesterday and meaningful to us today.

In 1966, Ron (Maulana) Karenga created Kwanzaa, the first Pan-African holiday, to honor African heritage in African American culture. Kwanzaa, observed from December 26 to January 1, culminates in a feast and gift giving. Covering eighty years of black life and history, culture, expression, and thought, *A Treasury of African American Christmas Stories*, captures the essence of the black experience in all its forms. It is a wonderful resource for those who celebrate both the traditional Christmas and Kwanzaa.

A Treasury of

AFRICAN AMERICAN

CHRISTMAS STORIES

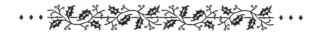

THE SERMON IN
THE CRADLE
W. E. B. Du Bois

"The Sermon in the Cradle," published in the *Crisis* in 1921, refers to Jesus Christ as "King of the Blacks." It was during the Harlem Renaissance era that African Americans became more vocal in challenging the notion and image of a white Christ. Using the Bible to authenticate their claims, biblical scholars, religious historians, and numerous writers produced books, pamphlets, poems, and other materials to publicize their assertions.

W. E. B. Du Bois, an original founder and incorporator of the NAACP, was a member of its board of directors, served as its director of publicity and research, and was the editor of its publication, the *Crisis* (1910–1934). During his long life and career (1868–1963), Du Bois was known as a teacher, author, editor, poet, scholar, and Pan-Africanist. A brilliant scholar and an intellectual with few peers, he graduated with a BA degree in 1885 from Fisk University. In 1888, he entered Harvard College, graduating BA cum laude in 1890 and receiving an MA degree in 1891. In 1895, he was awarded the PhD, the first African American to receive this degree from Harvard.

Du Bois was a prolific scholar, producing numerous books,

novels, pamphlets, poems, essays, and articles. His corpus of publications includes *The Philadelphia Negro* (1899), *The Souls of Black Folk* (1903), *The Quest of the Silver Fleece* (1911), *Darkwater: Voices Within the Veil* (1920), *The Gift of Black Folk: The Negroes in the Making of America* (1924), *Black Reconstruction in America* (1935), and seven autobiographical works.

The Sermon in the Cradle

ow when Jesus was born in Benin of Nigeria in the days of English rule, behold, there came wise men from the East to London.

Saying, where is he that is born King of the Blacks? For we have seen his star in the east, and are come to worship him.

When the Prime Minister had heard these things, he was troubled, and all England was with him.

And when he had gathered all the chief priests and scholars of the land together, he demanded of them where this new Christ should be born.

And they said unto him, in Benin of Nigeria: for thus it was written by the prophet:

And thou Benin, in the land of Nigeria, art not the least among the princes of Africa: for out of thee shall come a Governor that shall rule my Negro people.

Then the Prime Minister, when he had privately called the wise men, inquired of them diligently what time the star appeared.

And he sent them to Benin, and said, "Go and search diligently for the young child; and when ye have found him, bring me word again, that I may come and worship him also."

When they had heard the Premier, they departed; and lo, the star, which they saw in the east, went before them, till it came and stood over where the young child was.

When they saw the star, they rejoiced with exceeding great joy.

And when they were come into the house, they saw the young child with Mary his mother, and fell down, and worshiped him: and when they had opened their treasures, they presented unto him gifts: gold and medicine and perfume.

And being warned of God in a dream that they should not return to England, they departed into their own country another way.

Save one, and he was black. And his own country was the country where he was; so the black Wise Man lingered by the cradle and the new-born babe.

The perfume of his gift rose and filled the house until through it and afar came the dim form of years and multitudes. And the child, seeing the multitudes, opened his mouth and taught them, saying:

Blessed are poor folks for they shall go to heaven.
Blessed are sad folks for someone will bring them joy.
Blessed are they that submit to hurts for they shall sometime
    own the world.
Blessed are they that truly want to do right for they shall get
    their wish.
Blessed are those who do not seek revenge for
    vengeance will not seek them.
Blessed are the pure for they shall see God.
Blessed are those who will not fight for they are God's children.

*Blessed are those whom people like to injure for they shall
    sometime be happy.*
*Blessed are you, Black Folk, when men make fun of you and
    mob you and lie about you.*
Never mind and be glad for your day will surely come.
Always the world has ridiculed its better souls.

A CAROL OF COLOR

Mary Jenness

In the introduction to "A Carol of Color," Mary Jenness explained
that the poem was written from the point of view of people of color,
or "as the brown races see it." Pointing to the Christian tradition
made familiar by Ben Hur, she emphasized "that the three wise men
came from Egypt, India, and Greece; thus typifying the worship of
the Christ-child by the black, brown and white races." Published
in the magazine *Opportunity*, in the 1920s, during the Harlem
Renaissance, "A Carol of Color" asserts that Jesus Christ was
black. It was during that time that some African Americans began
to challenge the notion and image of a white Christ. Using biblical
scripture, which included, among other things, physical descriptions
of Christ, the argument was made that Christ was black.

In the early 1930s, *Opportunity* described Mary Jenness as an
"influential poet of the Harlem Renaissance." Among her most
celebrated poems were "The Negro Laughs Back" and "Secret."
Although we know little about Jenness, her "Carol of Color" reflects
the new African American ideology that emerged in the 1920s and
explains black history, religion, and color in a positive vein.

A Carol of Color

"I may not sleep in Bethlehem,
Your inns would turn me back—
Because," said Balthazar, unsmiling,
"My skin is black."

"I may not eat in Bethlehem,
Your inns would frown me down,
Because," said Melchior, uncomplaining,
"My skin is brown."

"Alone I ride to Bethlehem,
Alone I there alight,
Because," cried Gaspar, all unheeding,
"My skin is white."

Not one, nor two, but three they came,
To kneel at Bethlehem,
And there a brown-faced Christ-child, laughing,
Welcomed them.

THE CHRISTMAS REUNION DOWN AT MARTINSVILLE

Augustus M. Hodges

In "The Christmas Reunion Down at Martinsville," Augustus Hodges presents an African American version of a Christmas poem.

Hodges was a prominent New York writer, well known to readers of the major black newspapers, magazines, and journals of his time. In *The Afro-American Press, and Its Editors* (1891), I. Garland Penn stated, "He has few superiors in the journalistic field." Hodges's extensive news columns appeared regularly in black newspapers under his pen name "B. Square," and his poems, jokes, and short stories were widely represented in the leading black and white press of the time. A graduate of the Hampton Normal and Industrial Institute, Hodges distinguished himself as a politician, journalist, and fiction writer.

In 1876, Augustus Hodges was elected to the Virginia House of Delegates, where he served one term. During the 1890s, Hodges was a candidate for the position of US minister to Haiti, receiving the endorsement of more than five hundred leading Republicans. Failing to receive the appointment, Hodges continued to write and publish his fiction, and he served as a columnist for several black and white newspapers and periodicals, including the *Indianapolis*

Freeman and *Baltimore Afro-American*. In 1890, he established
the *Brooklyn Sentinel*, which for three years was considered one
of the leading African American newspapers in New York State.

In 1894, Hodges and several other black literary figures formed
a stock company known as the Augustus M. Hodges Literary
Syndicate to publish black novels and short stories in what he
described, in the *Indianapolis Freeman*, as "cheap paper-cover book
form." From 1894 to 1905, the *Freeman* purchased many of his
stories through this organization.

Hodges's stories reflect the full spectrum of black life and culture,
and incorporate his belief that "an author must use the words of
others in his song or story, and more especially if the said song or
story is a true one." Thus, his poems and stories, such as "The
Christmas Reunion Down at Martinsville" (1894), "The Blue and
the Gray" (1900), "Three Men and a Woman" (1902–1903),"
and "The Prodigal Daughter" (1904), mirror the beliefs, values,
speech, habits, and traditions of African Americans. Hodges prided
himself on the realism reflected in his writings. His fascination
and respect for the rich black vernacular expressions is evident in
all of his writings. In 1897, in a preface to " 'Twas Not to Be! Or
Cupid's Battle for Miscegenation," he stated that one of the motives
that prompted him to write was fame, and that if he reached his
goal, it would be "by facts, not fiction; by truth, not imagination."
Moreover, repeating Hodges's claim, one *Freeman* editor asserted,
"All of his novels are founded upon facts. The leading characters are
real and their doings real. Their names and locations have, however,
been changed; their doings painted with fiction and the links of the
events connected with the romantic imagination of the author, guided
by twenty odd years of careful study of the doings of both races."

"The Christmas Reunion Down at Martinsville" is set in Kentucky, around 1893. As three generations of a family gather to celebrate Christmas, Uncle Joe Moore, the narrator and patriarch, reminisces about how he and Aunt Sallie met some forty years earlier. Hodges presents the characters Uncle Joe and Sal as bound by the restrictions of slavery, particularly as it affected patterns of courtship and marriage. He demonstrates the types of risks enslaved men and women took to be together. Hodges also develops certain white characters, representatives primarily of the slaveholding class. The portrayal of Tom Scott, a patroller, suggests the surveillance and control exerted to police the movement of slaves to prevent their running away, the licentiousness of white men who showed no respect for the virtue of black women, and the problems black men encountered when they attempted to defend themselves or their women.

Hodges's white characters run the gamut from patroller and slave trader to preacher and the president of the United States. The first two are the embodiment of evil, and the last two are redeemed by their humanitarian acts. For a small price, the preacher willingly married slaves, and President Abraham Lincoln issued the Emancipation Proclamation, which presaged the freeing of the slaves.

Hodges also demonstrates the bravery of slaves who joined the Union army and fought in the Civil War. Utilizing Uncle Joe as narrator and having him reflect upon his and Sal's life as slaves and free persons allows Hodges to demonstrate the strong bond of love that some black men and women were able to develop. In describing the Christmas celebration as a reunion, he emphasizes the importance of family and tradition. And, finally, as Uncle Joe describes how his children worked hard to buy the land and build a house for their parents and how they succeeded in making a living, Hodges demonstrates that African Americans embraced the Protestant work ethic and worked together to ensure the success of their families.

The Christmas Reunion
Down at Martinsville

T was a bright Christmas morning in M "Old Kentucky,"
Aunt Sallie was busy disrobing a duck;
A featherless turkey close by her side lay,
Prepared for the dinner that bright Christmas day.
'Twas a family reunion, and Uncle Joe Moore
And his good wife, Aunt Sallie, both ten and three score,
Had gathered around them, their "girls" and their "boys,"
With their children's children—the grandparents toys.
The "girls" (all past thirty) were helping to make
The "sweet tater puddin's," the pies and the cake.
The "boys" and the grand boys, the fires were making,
The oldest granddaughter the biscuits were baking;
The little grandchildren, a dozen or more,
Were having a good time just outside the door;
While Uncle Joe Moore, the venerable sire,
Sat smoking his pipe, with his feet by the fire.
When the clock tolled the mid-day, the feast was complete,
And after each member had taken his seat,

The venerable sire stood up by his chair,
And with arms up-lifted he offered this prayer:
"We thank Thee, our Father in heaven," he said,
"For the abundance of good things before us now spread;
We thank Thee dear Lord, that me and my wife
Have been spared, by thy goodness, to reach an old life;
We thank Thee, of all things, the most and the best,
To meet all our children, from North, South and West.
Continue Thy blessings, Thy goodness and love,
And prepare us to meet Thee, in heaven above."
The grace being over, the feast was begun,
The duck and the turkey were carved one by one;
The big chicken pot-pie received the same fate,
A super-abundance was piled on each plate.
After the meats came the puddings and pies,
Then how the grandchildren all opened their eyes
When one of their uncles from up Illinois,
Brought out from the closet a basket of toys.
As dinner was over, the venerable sire,
Got up from his seat and stood by the fire.
He called to his side each lamb of his fold,
And blessed and caressed them, as Jacob of old.
"What changes we've seen Sal," remarked Uncle Joe,
"These years we've been married, some forty or so;
'Twas, let me see, forty? Yes, forty-one years
Since the Christmas we first met at Uncle Bill Stears.
I remember, ole 'oman, you looked mighty gran',
And I was then, children, a good lookin' man.
I walked with your mother from Clayton that night,

And 'fore we got home, why, I got in a fight;
Tom Scott, a patroller, insulted your mother,
And I knocked him down, and Ed., his big brother.
I then asked your mother if she'd be my wife.
Her answer was, "Yes Joe, since you risked your life
For me up the road, and licked ole Tom Scott—
Why, I'll be your wife, why Joseph why not?"
But the next day, my children, my master sold me
To an ole "nigger trader" from East Tennessee.
There I worked on a farm without seeing your mother
For eighty long days, 'till me and another
Plantation hand run away, and met with good luck,
For we soon found our self on the shores of Kentuck
Before my ole white folks knowed I run er way.
We two was married that same Christmas day.
We was married at Scottsville by ole Pete Brown,
He was a white preacher, who lived in the town,
And would marry we slave folks, no matter or not,
If our masters was willing, and if he only got
A two dollar bill, or a big barrel of corn:
And the very next Christmas our Lucy was born.
The next of the past that I now can remember,
Was when we moved here, Sal, the following September;
And then came the war, Sal, and old master died,
While Missus and you, Sal, stood by his side.
Then I left you and the children, and went out to fight
For the Union and freedom, one warm summer's night.
Then good Abraham Lincoln he set us all free,
And we had in Martinsville, a big jubilee;

Then you boys and you girls all worked hand to hand,
To buy me and your mother this house and this land.
Then some of you married, and some went out West,
While me and your mother, along with the rest,
Stayed on the old homestead and worked night and day,
A farming and trucking, and made the work pay.
We are glad for to meet you all back here once more,
And see all your dear babies together, before
Me and your mother, for we're both old and gray,
Receive old death's summons to call us away.
"God bless you and keep you through life, is my prayer,"
And the venerable sire sat down in his chair.
The rest of the evening was spent in a measure,
Receiving old friends, or by chatting in pleasure
Till long after midnight, with hearts light and gay—
'Twas a happy reunion, a bright Christmas day.

THE CHILDREN'S
CHRISTMAS

Alice Moore Dunbar

Educator, author, and social and political activist, Alice Moore
Dunbar received her first recognition as the wife of celebrated
poet and novelist Paul Laurence Dunbar and was later acclaimed
as a Harlem Renaissance poet. Born in New Orleans, Louisiana,
on July 19, 1875, Alice Ruth Moore was one of two daughters
of Joseph Moore, a Creole seaman, and Patricia Wright Moore.
She attended elementary and high school in New Orleans and
graduated from the two-year teacher training program at Straight
College (now Dillard University). She later studied at Cornell and
Columbia Universities and the University of Pennsylvania, where
she specialized in psychology and English educational testing.
Beginning her teaching career in New Orleans in 1892, except for
brief interruptions, she taught school for almost four decades.

In 1895, Alice Moore completed her first book, *Violets and
Other Tales*, and began a romance with Paul Laurence Dunbar,
who gained great fame for his Negro dialect verse. In 1897, she
moved from Boston to New York City, where she accepted a public
school teaching position in Brooklyn, and assisted Victoria Earle
Matthews in establishing in Harlem the White Rose Mission,
a home for girls. It was in December 1897 that she wrote "The

Children's Christmas," a story that reflected the lives of the children she taught.

"The Children's Christmas" is the story of five children, from different racial and ethnic backgrounds, who live in a large city. These children represent all children who, through circumstances not of their making, do not experience the joy, the spirit, and the meaning of Christmas. This social commentary by Moore is presented as a panorama to show how many children at the turn of the century did not celebrate the "luxury" of a real Christmas.

Julia is an unkempt seven-year-old who attends school mostly in the afternoon to reduce the necessity for breakfast. She lives with her mother, who drinks excessively and physically abuses her. When asked, "What will Santa bring you?" she replies, "Nothin' but another beatin'." Although Moore does not identify the child as being African American, the use of dialect suggests that she is.

Matilda is a Jewish girl who attends the same school as Julia. She lives in an orphanage. Being Jewish, she does not celebrate the holiday, but she accepts Santa Claus and the traditional role he plays. Santa brings toys, and Matilda wants a doll for Christmas.

Florence is too young for school, so she gets to play outdoors during the day. She views Christmas as a cold, uncomfortable time of the year. Poorly dressed in hand-me-down clothes, toys would not be number one on her list for Santa.

Frank, the nursemaid to his baby brother, wanders with his charge through the streets taking in all the beautiful decorations and hoopla of the holiday season. He gazes in the store windows knowing that his wish for even one toy would be in vain. Santa Claus would not stop by his house.

Hattie, almost blind since the age of six, cannot see the beautifully decorated store windows and other adornments of Christmas. But she can hear the joyful talk and sounds of the season. Is her wish for Christmas the gift of seeing?

Moore reminds the readers that Christmas is the children's time and that, regardless of race, ethnicity, gender, religion, or circumstance, all children should be given the opportunity to participate in this joyous occasion. She reminds the more fortunate in society that they should live up to the true spirit of Christmas and share their good fortune with those who are less fortunate.

It is most likely that the setting for this story is Brooklyn, New York, in 1897, the year that Alice Ruth Moore taught in a public school there. Moore, who was only twenty-two at the time the story was written, was struck with the plight of these children. Her concluding statement—"these little folks are not imaginary small personages created for Sunday-school literature and sentimental dissertations on so-called sociology. They are actual, evident, their counterparts around us, no matter where we may live"—suggests that she wrote the story to illustrate the plight of many urban children who lived in poverty and despair. As a budding young crusader, she embodied the spirit of the Progressive Era (1890–1920) and believed that one should use all resources to bring public attention to the conditions that existed in society.

The Children's Christmas

With the tinkle of joy-bells in the air, the redolence of pine and the untasted anticipation of saccharine joys to be, the child steps forward into the full heyday of his prerogatives. For this is childhood's time—it is the commemoration of a child's birth and the gifts brought him. It is a time of peace and gladness, say the children; it is our reign of love and gift-giving.

Yet even the small kings and queens who reign over this carnival of joy are not happy. There are many who have never come into their kingdom at all—to whom the luxury of a real Christmas would be a foretaste of Paradise. Did you ever stop to think of this? You who are pushing and jostling in the shopping crowd, your arms full of expensive toys, and your heart full of cheery cares lest someone be forgotten? We might have a little panorama for your especial benefit if you do not mind.

Julia is in school. She is seven and as unkempt as the school authorities will permit her. She is frequently absent from the morning session. We wondered why until we learned that her mother was "mos' all the time drunk" and didn't get up mornings, so Julia slept too to reduce the necessity for breakfast and came straggling in, in the afternoon, half stupid, wholly indifferent.

"What will Santa bring you?" asked her nearest neighbor in school during a lively discussion about Christmas.

She shrugged her tiny shoulders, "Nothin' but another beatin' I guess." And the nearest neighbor turned away to tell her chosen friend that as she had four dolls now she didn't want another one just yet.

Matilda is in the same school. She is a swarthy, pretty black-eyed Hebrew. Her black locks are cropped short. She wears the uniform of an asylum not far away. Christmas? It is incomprehensible to her. Who was the Christ child? Why keep his birthday? But Santa Klaus she understands, and the gifts that are denied her. Dolls! Why to possess even the tiniest one would seem too much happiness for a mortal Hebrew maiden. As she heard the other children enumerating their toys it seemed to her wonderful that they did not unfurl wings, for surely angels are so blessed. Why if she only had the wee smallest toy she would never need to speak in school again, so complete would be the measure of her bliss.

Florence is on the other side of the river and too small to be in school. So when it is warm she plays in the sunshine which freely attempts to clear the stagnant atmosphere. When the winds nip through from river to river she seeks shelter in a tenement, dark and fetid and noisy with brawls and drunkenness. Christmas? It means cold weather and shivering in a poor, thin jacket whose warmth was a thing of the past when it fell to her two years ago. Toys? Once she actually touched the dress of a gorgeously dressed lady doll, and the memory of it was like wine for weeks. Even now she regarded that hand in some measure as sacred.

Frank stands musingly before a window resplendent with gold and silver Christmas tree "fixin's." The poor child gazing hungrily in brilliant windows at holiday time is a figure that is well-nigh threadbare in juvenile fiction, but it is so pitifully, painfully true and ever-recurring. He clutches his baby brother by the arm and dreamfully wonders if there was ever one person on earth who was rich enough to buy all that. Baby brother grows impatient, for he is whimsical, and nurse Frank moves away signing hopelessly. It was like longing for ice cream the year round to even dare wish for one toy.

Hattie listens to the Christmas talk and the Christmas noise and the fakir's wondrous stream of unchecked gab, and wrinkles her little face painfully. You see she is almost blind, and subjects are but an indistinct blur to her. Blind at six, through carelessness and ignorance, with not a helping hand, that will lead her to a dispensary for treatment. She cannot see the wondrous windows; she can only hear and wonder. Who knows if in her groping, mental as well as physical, there does not form the faultily famed wish for the Christmas present of seeing?

These little folks are not imaginary small personages created for Sunday-school literature and sentimental dissertations on so-called sociology. They are actual, evident, their counterparts around us, no matter where we may live. They have been robbed of the most precious birthright that Heaven bestows—their childhood—and their annual birth-feast is denied them not because the world wishes them ill, but because the world is scarcely cognizant of their existence. And yet "Christmas is the children's time, the day of their rejoicing." Does it seem fair that to the least of them there does not filter some minute molecule of the general happiness, some infinitesimal spangled toy that would never be missed from the more fortunate ones?

CHRISTMAS EVE STORY

Fanny Jackson Coppin

A well-known educator, civic and religious activist, and feminist, Fanny Muriel Jackson was born enslaved in Washington, DC. Her freedom was purchased by Sarah Clark, her aunt. At a relatively young age, she was sent to live with another aunt in New Bedford, Massachusetts, where she worked as a domestic. At the age of fourteen she moved to Newport, Rhode Island, where she was employed for six years as a servant in the home of George Henry Calvert, a writer and the great-grandson of Lord Baltimore, who settled Maryland. In *Reminiscences of School Life, and Hints on Teaching*, Jackson wrote that it was during those years that she attended public school and became determined to "get an education and become a teacher of my people."

Fanny Jackson passed the entrance examination and was admitted to the Rhode Island State Normal School at Bristol, where she excelled. Following graduation, she was accepted by Oberlin College, one of the few white institutions of higher learning that admitted African Americans. At Oberlin, she pursued the classical course, known as the gentleman's course of study. The college did not prevent women from taking the classical course but did not advise it. As the course emphasized Latin, Greek, and mathematics, it was felt that women would not fare well.

Following her graduation from Oberlin, in 1865, Fanny accepted an appointment to teach at the Institute for Colored Youth, a school established in Philadelphia in 1837 by the Quakers. During the antebellum period, this school developed a reputation for excellent teachers, a classical curriculum, and the high quality of its graduates. The institute was a showplace, visited by interested persons from throughout the United States and Europe.

Contrary to the belief of many whites that blacks were inferior and suited only for menial labor, the Institute for Colored Youth proved that African Americans were quite capable of learning and could acquire a higher level of education. Fanny taught Greek, Latin, and mathematics, and served as principal of the girls' high school department. She was delighted to teach children and see them master Caesar, Virgil, Cicero, Horace, and Xenophon's *Anabasis*.

In 1869, the general principal of the institute, Ebenezer D. Bassett, was appointed minister to Haiti by President Ulysses S. Grant. Fanny Jackson replaced him as head principal, becoming the first black woman in the US to hold a position at that level in an educational institution. During her thirty-seven-year tenure at the institute, several students—future black leaders—came under Jackson's tutelage, and she was influential in shaping some of the major patterns of black education in the late nineteenth century.

In 1881, Fanny married the Reverend Levi Jenkins Coppin, a noted minister and bishop of the African Methodist Episcopal Church (AME). Although she held membership in a Baptist church, Mrs. Coppin became involved in the AME Church, and she was active in the missionary field and as president of the

Women's Home and Foreign Missionary Society. In 1888, she was a delegate to the Centenary Conference on the Protestant Missions of the World, held in London. At that meeting she spoke forcefully about the intelligence of African American women and the tremendous responsibilities they assumed in every endeavor, including missions. In 1893, she delivered the same message at the Chicago World's Fair.

Although she is best remembered for her work in education, Fanny Jackson was also widely known as a writer, lecturer, and organizer in the black women's club movement. "Christmas Eve Story" reflects her concerns for poor black children and illustrates the plight of many she came in daily contact with in the alleys and hovels where they resided in Philadelphia. This short story is written in the style of a fairy tale with an appeal to very young readers and listeners. It opens on Christmas Eve, 1879, and concludes on Christmas Eve, 1880. The references to Acorn Alley and the almshouse suggest a large city, most likely Philadelphia, where Fanny Jackson Coppin resided.

"Christmas Eve Story" was published in December 1880 in the *Christian Recorder*, the organ of the AME Church and one of the earliest black publications to publish the literary efforts of African Americans. Its diverse offerings attracted wide readership among black Methodists and appealed to a broad-based national African American audience. The story makes an appeal for the community to address the poverty experienced by so many black children who lived in filthy alleys infested with disease.

Christmas Eve Story

Once upon time, there was a little girl named Maggie Devins, and she had a brother named Johnny, just one year older than she. Here they both are. Now if they could they would get up and make you a bow. But dear me! We all get so fastened down in pictures that we have to keep as quiet as mice, or we'd tear the paper all to pieces. I'm going to tell you something about this little boy and girl, and perhaps some little reader will remember it. You see how very clean and neat both of them look. Well, if you had seen them when Grandma Devins first found them you never would have thought that they could be made to look as nice as this. Now hear their story:

Last Christmas Eve while Grandma Devins was sitting by her bright fire there was a loud knock at the door, and upon opening it, she found a policeman who had in his arms two children who were nearly dead.

"I come, mum," he said, "to ask you, if you will let these poor little young ones stay here to-night in your kitchen; their mother has just died from the fever. She lived in an old hovel around in Acorn Alley, and I'm afraid to leave the young ones there to-night, for they're half starved and half frozen to death now. God pity the poor, mum, God pity the poor, for it's hard upon then, such weather as this."

Meanwhile, Grandma Devins had pulled her big sofa up to the fire and was standing looking down upon the dirty and pinched little faces before her. She didn't say anything, but she just kept looking at the children and wiping her eyes and blowing her nose. All at once she turned around as if she had been shot; she flew to the pantry and brought out some milk which she put on the fire to boil. And very soon she had two steaming cups of hot milk with nice biscuit broken into it, and with this she fed the poor little creatures until a little color came into their faces, and she knew that she had given them enough for that time.

The policeman said he would call for the children in the morning and take them to the almshouse. The fact is the policeman was a kindhearted man, and he secretly hoped that he could get someone to take the children and be kind to them.

As soon as Maggie and Johnny had their nice warm milk they began to talk. Johnny asked Grandma Devins if she had anybody to give her Christmas presents, and Grandma said, "no." But Maggie spoke up and said her mamma told her before she died that God always gave Christmas presents to those who had no one to give them any. And throwing her arms around Grandma's neck she said, "God will not forget you, dear lady, for you've been so good to us." Like a flash of light it passed through Grandma Devins' mind that God had sent her these children as her Christmas gift. So she said at once:

"Children, I made a mistake. I *have* had a Christmas present."

"There," said Maggie, "I knew you would get one; I knew it." When the policeman came in the morning his heart was overjoyed to see the "young ones," as he called them, nicely washed and sitting by the fire bundled up in some of Grandma Devins' dresses. She had burnt every stitch of the dirty rags which they had on the night before. So that accounted for their being muffled up so.

"You can go right away, policeman; these children are my Christmas gift, and please God I'll be mother and father both to the poor little orphans."

A year has passed since then, and she says that Johnny and Maggie are the best Christmas gifts that any old woman ever had. She has taught Maggie to darn and sew neatly, and one of these days she will be able to earn money as a seamstress. Have you noticed her little needle-case hanging against the wall? Do you see the basket of apples on one side? Johnny was paring them when Maggie asked him to show her about her arithmetic, for Johnny goes to school, but Maggie stays at home and helps Grandma. Now as soon as Grandma comes back she is going to make them some mince pies for Christmas. Johnny will finish paring the apples, while Maggie is stoning the raisins. Oh! What a happy time they will have to-morrow. For I will whisper in your ear, little reader, that Grandma Devins is going to bring home something else with her other than raisins. The same kindhearted policeman who I told you about in the beginning, has made Johnny a beautiful sled, and painted the name "Hero" on it. Grandma has bought for Maggie the nicest little hood and cloak that ever you saw. Is that not nice? I guess if they knew what they're going to get they wouldn't sit so quietly as we see them; they'd jump up and dance about the floor, even if they tore the paper all to pieces. Oh! Let every little girl [and boy] thank our heavenly father for the blessed gift of His dear Son on the first Christmas Day, eighteen hundred and eighty years ago.

MOLLIE'S BEST
CHRISTMAS GIFT

Mary E. Lee

Mary E. Lee, the daughter of Simon S. and Adelia M. Ashe, was born free in Mobile, Alabama, on January 12, 1851. In 1860, the family moved to Xenia, Ohio, the site of Wilberforce University, one of the first institutions of higher learning to be established for African Americans in the United States. Founded by the African Methodist Episcopal Church (AME), Wilberforce included what was known as a "normal" department, which provided primary and secondary instruction for black children and adults in addition to the college course. Lee attended Wilberforce and graduated with a BS degree in 1873. As a student, she distinguished herself as a poet and essayist, and after graduation, she taught in the public schools of Galveston, Texas. In December 1873, she married Benjamin Franklin Lee, president of Wilberforce and a professor of theology. In 1892, he was elected a bishop of the AME Church.

During the late nineteenth century, Mary E. Lee was well known as a poet, fiction writer, and religious worker in the AME Church. Her articles, poems, and short stories appeared in the *Christian Recorder*, *AME Quarterly Review*, *Ringwood's Journal*, and other publications. During the 1890s, the Lee family resided in Philadelphia, where Mary was affiliated with the Women's Christian

Temperance Union, the Ladies' Christian Union Association, and the AME Women's Mite Missionary Society. In 1892, she was elected vice president of the Afro-American Press Association.

"Mollie's Best Christmas Gift" was published in the *Christian Recorder* in December 1882. Lee wrote the story to emphasize the importance of putting Christ back in Christmas. The Christmas celebration, introduced in the United States during the late eighteenth century, was officially recognized by most states as a legal holiday by 1865. By 1850, the celebration had taken on its more modern character, with feasting and gift giving being the foremost focus. Lee's concern in 1885 is echoed today by many, especially parents who are besieged by children who view Christmas simply as a time to receive toys and presents.

"Mollie's Best Christmas Gift" not only imparts a message for Christians, but it also provides the reader with a glimpse of what Christmas was like for middle-class black children in the late nineteenth century.

Raised as a free black child of privilege, Mary Lee spoke from experience. Little is known about the reading and recreational habits of black children in the late nineteenth century, but in this story, we learn that they read traditional US history books such as *The Pilgrim's Progress* and *Line upon Line* and fairy tales including "Cinderella," "Puss in Boots," and "Beauty and the Beast."

Lee's message in "Mollie's Best Christmas Gift" is simple yet profound. It is that Christmas is about the birth of the Christ child and that the best present a child can receive is the Bible, which provides one the opportunity to know and to understand the teachings of Jesus.

✯ ✯ ✯ ✯ ✯

Mollie's Best Christmas Gift

ollie's parents had been "well-to-do," and she had always looked forward to Christmas as a day of joy and merriment. She awoke Christmas morning to find her stockings filled or the Christmas tree laden with toys and good things. Among her presents were so many fairy stories, including of course, "Cinderella," "Puss in Boots," "Beauty and the Beast," etc. She also had "Line upon Line" and "Pilgrim's Progress." A week before the Christmas in which our story begins, Mollie had been trying to decide in her mind what she would like to get on Christmas as a present. She had almost every kind of toy, so she could think of nothing new that she had not had on previous holidays. She consoled herself with the hope that her parents and friends would think of something new and beautiful. But the circumstances of her parents had changed; her father found himself less able than he had ever been before to provide many presents for the children so he concluded to buy only such things as would be useful.

Mollie, herself, was somewhat changed from what she had been on other Christmases. She was older now and more thoughtful. She had a restlessness [which she did not understand], a feeling that there was some duty she had neglected, with an undefined desire for something which she might have attained, but had not. Thus she looked forward to Christmas. What was her chagrin when she found that her presents consisted of only a pair of shoes, a dress and a silver dollar! She was so greatly disappointed in receiving what she considered no present—only the things necessary to her comfort, which her father would provide for her at any time—that she hid her face in the folds of her blue merino dress to conceal her tears; then looking around she saw under the mantle a parcel addressed thus "To Mollie from her brother, Joseph." It contained a book, "The Prince of the House of David." She began that day to read her book and carefully read it with growing interest in the history day by day. Of course she had long since learned the story of the cross, both at home and at the Sunday school, though she had not felt that she had a personal concern in it. But in reading this book, Jesus of Nazareth appeared to her the fairest among ten thousand and altogether lovely. Yet she thought the book might not be true. Perhaps, these letters were not written by the Alexandrian maiden, after all. But, she [told herself], "The Bible tells the story. I will read my Testament." So she began to read the story of Jesus in her Testament as she had never read it before. There was new light upon the pages as she read; light grew lighter and lighter until her heart seemed to run over with love and sympathy for Christ and to melt with shame at her own unworthiness.

It was New Year's morning; for one week she had been reading and thinking of Jesus, and her Christmas gifts resulted in the happiest New Year she can ever have on earth, for then she first received Jesus, the hope of earth and joy of heaven, as her Saviour. Ever since then she has felt like saying to little girls and boys just giving up their childish toys, "Remember now thy Creator in the days of thy youth."

A CHRISTMAS STORY

Carrie Jane Thomas

"A Christmas Story," published in the *Christian Recorder* in 1883, is a traditional children's fable with mystical characters and magical events, including the mythical Santa Claus. It is a moral parable whose message to children is to be good and obedient to your parents and believe in Santa Claus, and all your wishes will be granted.

The story focuses on Minnie Leslie, a ten-year-old girl, one of four children who live with her parents in comfortable middle-class surroundings. The Leslie children have been encouraged to believe in Santa Claus and have been warned that if they are disobedient he will not leave them toys and gifts. Minnie, influenced by Lucy, a girlfriend, determines to stay awake to see Santa Claus and to dispute the claims of Lucy, who argues that Santa Claus is none other than Minnie's parents.

Although little is known about Carrie Jane Thomas, she obviously was interested in writing children's literature. "A Christmas Story" was written for middle-class black children, whose expectations of Santa Claus and Christmas paralleled those of their white counterparts. Unlike the Santa Claus depicted fifty years later by Langston Hughes in "One Christmas Eve," and John Henrik Clarke in "Santa Claus Is a White Man," Thomas's traditional Santa Claus is universal in his love for all children. He could, and did, serve the purpose of middle-class parents, who used him as a kind of surrogate parent to maintain discipline and instill important values in their children.

A Christmas Story

It is Christmas night and Mr. and Mrs. Leslie are seated in their cozy parlor surrounded by their four children, Kittie, Susie, Willie, and Minnie, who is papa's pet and allowed to do almost as she pleases. They are talking about the one thing Christmas brings—Santa Claus—each busy telling what is wanted. They keep such chattering you can scarcely hear your ears. When Mr. Leslie says, "children, it is ten o'clock," all the noise is stopped at once and their faces become very sad, for they all know that it is their bedtime, and, knowing their father's rules, not one dares protest, although the time has passed unusually quick. At last the silence is broken by "Pet" [Minnie].

"I am not going to bed at all tonight, papa; I am determined to see Santa Claus this night, for Lucy Bennett told me, when we were coming from school, that ma and pa were the Santa Claus and they put all the things into our stockings; but I told her I did not believe it. I am ten years old and never saw Santa Claus in my whole life, so I shall sit up all night."

"Well, you won't get anything," says Kittie.

"I don't care for anything, but to see Santa Claus," [answers Minnie].

Her mama smiled and said, "I am afraid my little girl could not bear the sight of Santa, even if she could stay awake until he comes, which is very doubtful."

"I know he won't give you anything, cause you is so quisitive," says Willie. "All the reason you gets anything is because he feels sorry for a poor tongue-tied boy like you that can't talk plain," [responds Minnie].

"You won't be so fierce in the morning, when you begin to beg," retorts Willie.

"Willie!" calls his mother, "you ought to be ashamed of yourself to tease your sister so; go to bed this moment."

All of the children trooped off to bed. Mama and papa went up to their room, leaving poor Minnie all alone. "As the stockings were all hung in the parlor," Minnie says to herself, "he is obliged to pass through here and I will sit close to my own stocking so I can see when he goes to put the goodies in." Minnie exclaims, as she hears the clock strike eleven, "I am so glad it is eleven, I won't have to wait long. They say he always comes at twelve." If poor Minnie had known what she was destined to see at twelve, she would have gone to bed. But she did not, and so the time goes by and it is almost twelve o'clock. Minnie is so sleepy. She looks at the clock, only a quarter to twelve. "I cannot go to sleep. I must see him, and, besides, how they will laugh when I tell them I got sleepy and could not wait." Just then she goes off, and the clock strikes twelve. The door opens and in walks Santa Claus, followed by twenty of his confederates. Santa Claus himself is a little fat man with white, bushy beard and white hair covered with a frost of many winters. He has a doll for Kittie, a horse and wagon for [Willie], dresses for Sue, and, in fact, everything they all wanted, but for Minnie he had nothing. Minnie began to whimper.

"What is the matter?" asks Santa, in a gruff voice, as if he had just seen her.

"I want something, too."

"There will be more than you want presently," and he proceeded to fill the stockings. When he had filled all but Minnie's, he gave a whistle and marched through the room and passed out, followed by another whom she had not seen. His name was on his cap and Minnie saw that it was Disobedience. He was loaded with articles of every description. Minnie saw her blue silk dress, which she remembered wearing to an evening party when her mother told her not to do so. Then there was her last birthday present, a silver cup from papa, which her mother told her never to carry to the spring, but she disobeyed and dropped it into the spring. There were many other things, too numerous to mention. All this Minnie took in at a glance. He passed on and another took his place; he had scraps of rick-rack, crochet, and knitting dangling from head to foot; he also carried a box in his hand which was filled with dolls' clothes, dresses and aprons without sleeves and without hems; there were the mittens she promised to Widow James, but never finished. He passed on and another came in with Minnie's books, torn and scratched, with dolls' heads, and crippled men and women drawn on them, which would make you laugh to see. The next had half worn shoes and stockings, which might have been given to some poor children, but Minnie had allowed them to lie around out of doors until they were unfit for use. Another came in making such horrible faces that Minnie covers her face with her hands and begins to scream, which awakens her to find that she has only been dreaming. She is as cold as she can be, for the fire has gone out and the room is dark. Minnie jumps up and goes to bed, where Kittie has been for at least three hours. Next morning the children were up searching their stockings, which were filled with everything they had asked for, and to Willie's surprise, Minnie's stocking was overflowing. You may be sure that was a memorable Christmas [for] Minnie, and I need not tell you that she is over forty years old and she has never tried waiting for Santa Claus again.

FANNIE MAY'S CHRISTMAS

Katherine Davis Tillman

Katherine Davis Chapman Tillman was born in Mound City, Illinois, on February 19, 1870, and at an early age she evidenced a special talent for writing. Encouraged by her mother, a gifted teacher and writer, she soon gained a reputation as a poet. In 1888, the *Christian Recorder* published "Memory," her first poem. Her first short story appeared in *Our Women and Children* magazine, published by the American Baptist Publication Society. She soon became famous for her poetry and prose, which appeared in all the leading black newspapers and periodicals.

A graduate of the Yankton High School in South Dakota, she also attended the state university at Louisville, Kentucky, and Wilberforce University. Around 1890, she married George M. Tillman, an African Methodist Episcopal (AME) minister. As a Christian feminist activist, Tillman was editor of the *Women's Missionary Recorder* and served as secretary of the Iowa Branch of the Women's Mite Missionary Society for twelve years and as president of the North Missouri AME Conference Branch. Like many female church leaders, she was active in the National Association of Colored Women (NACW). Tillman was honorary president of the City Federation of Colorado Springs and honorary president of the California Federation. As the director of the

Baby Department of the NACW's Public Posters and Prints, she monitored the publication and distribution of posters and prints illustrating negative images and derogatory caricatures of African American children. In 1919, she targeted the Gold Dust Twins, a popular and highly successful caricature of black children who were depicted in a variety of comical and demeaning antics on posters, playing cards, and other products. Tillman organized clubs throughout the United States to protest the N. K. Fairbank Company, the distributors of the materials. Although she did not succeed in having the products removed from the market, the firm toned down the images.

Tillman, an ardent feminist, stated in an 1893 *AME Church Review* article entitled "Some Girls That I Know," that "there is one phase of my literary career that I thoroughly enjoy, and that is the privilege of writing to the young women of my race. Sometimes I address myself to them in stories, as in 'Our Ruth,' sometimes in poetry, but always I have an earnest desire to reach them and help them." And so, in 1921, she wrote "Fannie May's Christmas," which was published in the *Christian Recorder*. The sub-theme of this short story is gender issues.

"Fannie May's Christmas" is set in 1877 in Louisville, Kentucky. Eight-year-old Fannie May, the only child of a poor but hard-working family, has been informed that Santa probably will not visit her for Christmas because times are too hard and her mother is ill.

Under these dire circumstances, Fannie May and her family, together with friends and church members, work hard to make gifts and prepare goodies to share at Christmas. Through these efforts and another blessed event, the true meaning of Christmas is discovered and celebrated by Fannie May and her community.

✱ ✱ ✱ ✱ ✱

Fannie May's Christmas

It was a long time ago, for it was in 1877 that Fannie May, a dear little girl with brown face and long, silky braids of hair, of which she was very proud when it was properly beribboned, lived on York Street in the city of Louisville [Kentucky]. In addition to her beautiful hair, Fannie May had other attractions. She had bright, black eyes that seemed ever to hold a smile lurking in their depths and a disposition that made her loved from one end of the street in which she lived to the other.

Fannie May's father worked across the street, in the big tobacco factory on the corner where he and a hundred others of Negro-American ancestry stemmed and packed tobacco for shipping.

Fannie May's mother, a fair little woman of frail physique, worked for a kind white family when she was able. Living was very high in this beautiful Southern city, and when Fannie May's father had paid the exorbitant rent demanded by his white landlord for their two-room home, kept fire in the kitchen stove, and in the grate fire place in the living room, bought wood and the cheapest kind of clothing, there was very little left of the seven dollars and a half pay that he received each week. Then, too, as her father would have told you himself, he was a typical Kentuckian of that day, and a laboring man must have his morning toddy, and the little store on the corner with its bar in the rear sometimes got a third of his week's pay.

So you see when Fannie May's mother was ailing as she had been now for several weeks and could not go to work for her "white folks," it looked mighty, mighty, slim for Christmas doings at Fannie May's humble little home.

And since there were just two things, out of all the things in the whole round world, that Fannie May had set her heart on, it did seem as if a little girl who didn't act greedy and ask for lots and lots of things like May Bell and Prudie Ann, two of her little friends, might have those two things.

But while Fannie May was only eight, she had lots of sense, and Grannie Hope, who lived next door, always declared she was "old in the head," because she was so thoughtful.

She spoke of these two things as she ate her share of corncake and sorghum at supper.

"I just wish Santy Claus would bring me just two things out of all the millions of things he's got in his sleigh," she sighed.

"What's that, Fannie May?" said her father, who was very fond of his little daughter.

"I wants a great big doll, that can shut its eyes and go to sleep when I rock it and say 'mamma' when you squeeze it; and then I wants a great big cradle bed, to put it to sleep in. Me and Prudie Ann and May Bell saw one [in] the store when we took the white folk's clothes home. Oh, pappy, it was just beautiful. If I had a big doll and bed, I wouldn't want another thing. All the other children get something to play with but me. I ain't got no little brother and sister, nor nothing 'tall."

Fannie May's father's face grew long. "Don't look for nothing this Christmas, cause I done heard tell Santa Claus wouldn't be able to get around to our place at all, cause times is so hard."

Fannie May's bright eyes filled with tears. "An I ain't going to get nothin 'tall," she said. "How come he ain't coming here this Christmas? He never missed before?"

"Times too hard and mamma's sick."

"I would got something off the Sunday-school Christmas tree, but I done missed fo' Sundays staying with mamma, and when you done missed fo' Sundays, Prudie Ann and May Bell both say you don't get nothin' off the Christmas tree," and overwhelmed by the tragic turn of affairs Fannie May wept aloud.

Fannie May's mother, who was in bed, roused right up. She always did, if there was anything the matter with Fannie May. Mothers are like that, you know.

"Stop crying! Mother's child," she said. "Indeed, you will have something for Christmas, soon as I feel the least bit better; I'll begin right away making some new Christmas clothes for Ella Virginia."

Fannie May's most cherished possession was a big rag doll, made by her mother out of flour sacking and stuffed with bran from a neighboring lumber yard. Her face was outlined with bluing and on her head was real hair, cut from Fannie May's mother's head. Ella Virginia had been Fannie May's pride since she was five. She shared all of her games of play-house and was hugged close to her bosom when Fannie May went to sleep, but constant wear with an active little mistress like Fannie May had reduced Ella Virginia to a mere wreck of her former self. She had leaky arms and legs. Her face was so soiled that it was hard to discover where [her] eyes had been, and even Fannie May's loving heart ached at the sorry appearance of Ella Virginia beside the china dolls owned by Prudie Ann and May Bell.

The last time the trio had a sewing bee for their doll children, over in Prudie Ann's back yard, Fannie May's friends had so openly poked fun at Ella Virginia that the little mother had arisen in righteous wrath and hied herself homeward—her eyes filled with angry tears—but the sad fact remained unchanged—Ella Virginia's best days were past. She could still be loved and played with alone at home—but out, never! Still it would not be fair to Ella Virginia to refuse new clothes for her. Her mother could make such a cunning little jacket and such pretty dresses for Ella Virginia, and she worked real button holes in her clothes, and Fannie May could button them just as she did her own clothing.

She assented tearfully and went about her dishes as cheerfully as she could, but her little heart was sad, oh so sad, because she of all the little girls in her street would have no visit from Santa Claus at Sunday school or at home.

When Fannie May's last dish was washed and placed upon the cupboard shelves and she had read a chapter in the New Testament, with her father she sat in her own little red rocker that her father's kind dark hands had made for her on her last birthday, and looked in the big fire place and imagined how wonderful it would be if on Christmas Eve she could hang her stocking up, just as she did last Christmas, and wake up and find it all crammed to the toe with good things—candy and nuts and a big yellow orange from far-away Florida or California, and a big doll and a sure-enough cradle-bed, big enough to put her to sleep in, and—but the little eyes had closed, for the Sandman had managed to throw a good, big handful of sand in them, I suppose, and Fannie May trembled out of the little red rocker to the floor and her father picked her up and kissed her and put her to bed.

When he was through, Fannie May's mother was crying, for she had been watching Fannie May, and she knew what she was thinking about, for she knew what she thought about at Christmas time when she was like Fannie May and she knew that it breaks a child's heart when she is told to expect nothing for Christmas.

"Billie Boy, Fannie May's so little. She don't know anything about hard times. She must have a Christmas. Oh, and here I am sick and can't get out to work.

"Why, look here! It isn't fair for a poor man like me to have two babies on his hands at once," [said Fannie's father,] with an awkward pat on his sick wife's head. "But don't worry; she shall have some Christmas if I have to set up every night for a month. I'm going to make her a doll cradle-bed, big enough for a sure-enough baby, just as she is fretting about. I've got some nice pine that will be just the thing and you can make the mattress between grunts," he added with a mischievous smile.

Fanny May's mother was young, so she clapped her thin brown hands together almost as Fannie May would have done. "And, Billie Boy, I can make the little sheets and pillow cases and tack a comfort. I'm so glad you thought of such a beautiful thing to do. I know it will be just fine, because you made Fannie May's little rocker so nice."

"Then, too," said Fannie May's father, his face all smiles, "you know Granny Hope's a powerful hand for molasses cookies and molasses candy, and we've got plenty of sorghum laid by, and if I can get hold of a few walnuts for the candy, I guess Fannie May'll feel pretty good after all, except for the doll and I don't see how we can manage that unless one drops down from the skies somewhere."

"Like the Babe of Bethlehem," sighed the mother. "Well, I'll do all I can to make Ella Virginia presentable."

Night after night found Fannie May's father sitting up after a hard day's work at the factory, working on the cradle-bed. Sometimes he would fall asleep at his task, but when he did, he always got up an hour earlier in the morning and made up for it. He had to hide it at Granny Hope's, next door, to keep Fannie May from knowing. At last it was finished, and when he brought it home after Fannie May was asleep, Fannie May's mother was too happy for anything. "Oh, how could you make such a beautiful, beautiful bed, all by yourself?" she said.

For the cradle bed was wonderfully carved with the figure of an angel at the head, and it had nice even slats and rockers just like a true bed.

"It is big enough for a real baby, sure enough," said the mother.

Then they began to plan again about the cookies and candy. Yes, Granny Hope would make them. Fannie May's mother had done her more than one good turn when she was down with her back, and they needn't bother one mite about the walnuts, for she had some nice, fresh ones her son had sent in from the country, and she would make walnut taffy like she used to make at the "Big Houses" at Christmas times, before the War. Of course she meant the Civil War that freed the American slaves.

Fannie May knew nothing of these delightful doings, but she was more cheerful than she had been for she was busy making presents for others. Out of an old red flannel shirt Granny Hope gave her, she made a needle case for her mother and stitched the edges with coarse black thread and a pen wiper for her father; then she made two iron holders for Granny and covered them with some scraps of ticking, and for Prudie Ann and May Bell she made the dearest little pin cushions. Did you know there was so much Christmas in a discarded red flannel shirt? Of course there was magic in Fanny May's little fingers, the magic of love, and we can all have that if we work hard enough for it.

You remember I told you that everybody liked Fannie May because of her pleasant disposition. Well, Prudie Ann and May Bell

and the day school teacher and the Sunday school teacher all missed
the bright eyed little one with the sunny smile, and when the children told the teachers how Fanny May's mother was sick, and Santa
Claus wouldn't be able to bring Fanny May not a speck of Christmas,
both of the teachers felt so sorry and said to themselves that something must really be done about it, for it really wasn't right for a little
girl who minded her parents and teachers and did her work well at
home and school and seldom ever pouted, should have to go without
Christmas. The day teacher, a young woman who had struggled very
hard to get through school herself, went to work that very day and began to crochet Fanny May the dearest little blue hood, just like all the
fortunate little girls were wearing that winter and then she ripped up
a blue skirt that she had outgrown, cleaned and pressed it and made
Fannie May a little blue cape to match the hood and bought and
sewed three shiny gold buttons down the front. The Sunday-school
teacher, who was a very busy woman with a big family of her own,
took time and went to see Fannie May's mother, to learn just exactly
what Santa Claus might be expected to do for Fannie May at Christmas. They had a nice visit, then the teacher saw the superintendent
and gave him the size of the little girl's shoes, and he said the Sunday-
school Santa Claus would be happy to put a nice new pair of shoes on
[the Christmas tree] for Fannie May, together with the regular treat,
and the teacher thanked him and bought a pair of stockings to go
with the shoes, and they [hung] them on the Christmas tree with two
hundred pink, red, yellow, white and blue bags of candy and nuts.

Christmas Eve night, the day teacher, who had the [hood] and
cape all done [and] tied up in nice, smelly paper, with a blue ribbon,
came by for Fannie May to go to the Christmas tree. It was the first
time she knew she was going to get to go.

"Oh! Oh!" she fairly screamed. "Going to the Christmas Tree! Going to the Christmas Tree! Got a new blue hood; got a new blue cape." She danced up and down with joy.

Her mother and day teacher were happy too. By and by, here came Prudie Ann and May Bell to see if Fannie May could go, and Oh, she could, and her silky braids looked so pretty under the new hood, and the cape was just right, and Oh, wasn't it just a beautiful world after all—a beautiful Christmas world!

At the church a wonderful Christmas tree sparkled with candles and gifts, and the superintendent told of the Babe of Bethlehem, in whose honor the gifts were made. There was a concert, two dialogues, songs and speeches about Christmas. The day teacher held the children spellbound with "The Night Before Christmas," and at the close, the gifts were distributed. Fannie May got a pair of shoes, stockings, a pink bag of candy, and a little china doll, jointly contributed by her two little friends. How happy she was when she took her things home, but when she rushed up to the door she found that mamma was not well enough to be disturbed, and that she was to sleep next door at Granny Hope's and her father added that Granny said she had better hang up her stocking for she had heard that Santa Claus might come by after all.

Fanny May didn't really mind staying with Granny, but she would rather have stayed home on this particular night to talk over all that had taken place. Over at Granny Hope's she snuggled under the warm Irish chain quilt and peeped out every little while to see if she could see any sign of Santa Claus, but alas, the Sandman got her and it was bright day when she heard Granny stirring, and jumping out of bed cried quickly, "Christmas Gift! Granny, Christmas Gift!"

"Oh, you caught me, did you, you little Booger," said Granny, and gave her a big red apple and then Fannie May rushed to the fire-place, for there was the stocking she had hung up the night before, fat and mysterious looking. In it she found molasses cookies, candy and a ginger-bread man.

Fannie May rushed into her clothes and hurried over home.

But what was that standing in the middle of the kitchen floor? A cradle-bed! The prettiest you ever saw, big enough for Ella Virginia, or a live baby and it had a mattress and pillows and the daintiest comforter imaginable.

"Oh, papa! Oh, mamma!" she cried, rushing into the other room, but she stopped still for her mother was taking medicine from a glass her father held and Granny, who had come in another way was holding something in her arms—something that looked like a doll—something tiny and brown and wrinkled, but Oh, so very dear—something that you loved the very minute you laid eyes on it, and wanted to hold it in your arms.

"Oh, mamma, it isn't a live baby, is it?" cried the happy child, as Granny laid it in her arms for a wee moment.

"Yes, it is your Christmas Gift—your own, dear, little baby brother! Will you let him lie in your cradle-bed when he is sleepy?"

"Oh, mamma! Oh, daddy!" cried Fannie May; "I thought I wasn't going to have any Christmas at all, and it's the best Christmas in the whole world, isn't it? Didn't God give us a good Christmas this time?"

ELSIE'S CHRISTMAS
Salem Tutt Whitney

Salem Tutt Whitney was born in Logansport, Indiana, in 1869. The oldest child of a struggling itinerant minister, at an early age he quit school for a short period of time to work. Eventually he graduated from Shortridge High School in Indianapolis and then attended DePauw University, where he studied for the ministry. Except for brief employment as the minister of a church in Titusville, Pennsylvania, Whitney enjoyed a distinguished career as a stage performer, playwright, producer, comedian, poet, and journalist. His first stage performance was in 1895, singing bass with the Puggsley Brothers' Tennessee Warblers, a minstrel company.

In 1899, Whitney formed a company, the Oriental Troubadours, an aggregation of twenty-eight people and a nine-piece band. He toured the country with this group for seven years. In 1901, he opened his first musical comedy, *The Ex-President of Liberia*. Whitney wrote the book and music, staged the entire show, arranged the numbers, and designed the costumes. His brother, J. Homer Tutt, was his understudy for this production. The two of them later made the name Tutt and Whitney famous. In 1905, he joined the S. H. Dudley Smart Set Company, and in 1907, Homer and Salem joined the Black Patti's Troubadours as Whitney

and Tutt, the beginning of the famous combination. A couple of
years later, in 1909, they organized the second company of the
original Smart Set Company, and in 1916, they gained control
of the company and renamed it Whitney and Tutt's Smarter Set
Company.

Between 1909 and 1922, Whitney wrote a big two-act musical
comedy for every theatrical season. From 1910 to 1914, the Smart
Set was one of only four major black road companies in the field.
Whitney and Tutt were a key link in the black show business world
between the famous Williams and Walker team, and Black Patti to
Irvin Miller and Billy King.

In "Elsie's Chrisunas," published by the *Indianapolis Freeman* in
1912, Salem Tutt Whitney tells the traditional story of Christmas
and the role of Santa Claus. He touches upon a number of issues
that confronted African American families by showing that the love
between black men and women can be strained by economic and
political forces outside of their control. He also emphasizes the
problems single women have when they must support their children
on their own. Thus Whitney argues for black men and women to
be more sensitive and understanding of each other's needs.

"Elsie's Christmas" could be set at any time and in any place.
However, Elsie's request for a doll with "the pretty brown face and
Indian hair," suggests that the story occurs at some point between
1908 and 1912. Although so-called Negro dolls were available
during the 1890s, most were produced by white factories and had
what some considered "uncomely and deformed features." In 1908,
the National Baptist Convention set the pace for production of
"Negro Doll Babies for Negro Children." The movement for
black dolls was one indication of the growing African American

race consciousness so evident during the first and second decades of the twentieth century, which became full-blown in the New Negro Movement of the 1920s. Although dolls with brown faces appeared, they all had straight hair or what Elsie calls "Indian hair."

In addition to reinforcing the theme of race pride, Whitney, in referring to the two female characters, Virgie and Elsie, as Mrs. Waterman and "little lady," subtly introduces the issue of respect for black womanhood. White Americans frequently addressed black men and women by their first names or called them "girls," "boys," "aunties," and "uncles." To negate this pattern of disrespect, blacks would not use their first names but would refer to themselves only as Mr. or Mrs. with their surname.

Elsie's mother, Mrs. Waterman, calls her daughter "little lady" as a pet name. As Whitney explains in the story, Mrs. Waterman "had also explained to her [Elsie] the full significance of the word 'lady,' and how important it was for her daughter to have all the requisites of a lady." This statement and the use of the term suggests that black women were concerned about the image of black womanhood, an issue used by Ida Wells Barnett and the National Association of Colored Women, to thwart the proliferation of negative images of African American women, who were frequently depicted by white leaders and the white press as being women of loose morals. Mrs. Waterman stressed to Elsie that if one is to be considered a lady she must conduct herself in that manner, meaning she must be refined and have "gentle manners" and must receive the "homage or devotion" of her husband or lover.

Finally, in the best of African American traditions, the story speaks of the power of prayer. Elsie was taught that if she "prayed to the Good Man for anything I really wanted or needed, and believed that He would give me what I asked for, He'd do it?" In the depths of slavery, when there seemingly was no hope, enslaved men and women also believed that God would answer their prayers. God answered Elsie's and Mrs. Waterman's prayers because they had been good and had faith.

Elsie's Christmas

"Mamma, how old is Santa Claus?"

Mrs. Waterman was making a melancholy inspection of her clean but meagerly furnished kitchen. She turned at the sound of Elsie's voice and looked at her youthful questioner. She noted the perfect oval of the little girl's face, the healthy color, the beautiful coal-black eyes and the dark brown hair curling rebelliously away from the intelligent forehead. As Mrs. Waterman made this rapid inventory of Elsie's charms, her face became suffused with a smile of motherly pride, in which love, tenderness, and solicitude were equally blended.

In the year that they had been alone, Mrs. Waterman had never grown used to Elsie's puzzling and startling questions. Elsie's mind seemed unusually matured for a girl six years of age. No matter how trivial the questions, Mrs. Waterman always considered them seriously, knowing that intelligent answers would help develop her daughter's intellect. So now, as she looked at Elsie's expectant face, she pondered her answer.

"Santa Claus is very old," she answered gravely; "very, very old, little Lady."

"Little Lady" was the pet name Mrs. Waterman had given her daughter. She had also explained to her the full significance of the word "lady," and how important it was for her daughter to have all the requisites of a lady. Elsie was very proud of the name.

"Is he as old as papa?" asked Elsie, after a childish attempt to compute the years necessary to make one very, very old.

At the word "papa" a pained expression came into Mrs. Waterman's face, but it was only momentary and passed unnoticed by Elsie.

"Very much older than your—papa," Mrs. Waterman answered, thoughtfully.

"I guess he must be older than grandpop, too," mused Elsie; "his hair looks whiter and his beard longer in the pictures I see of him. Did anybody ever see Santa Claus when he was little?"

"Yes," answered the mother.

"Who?" eagerly questioned Elsie.

"It is a story, little Lady," replied Mrs. Waterman.

"Oh! little mother, tell it to me, won't you, please?" pleaded Elsie.

Mrs. Waterman, glad of the opportunity to rest, seated herself in a chair near the window. Elsie climbed eagerly upon her knee, threw her chubby arms affectionately about her mother's neck and kissed her full upon the lips. With all the infinite love of a mother showing in her face, made radiant by the holiest of passions, Mrs. Waterman pressed the child to her bosom.

The winter's sun, like a golden globe of unquenchable fire, was sinking slowly below the horizon; its yellow rays smiled through the window and formed a halo around the little girl's head. A flood of tenderness swelled in the mother's bosom, bringing tears to her eyes, and she knew how the Virgin Mary must have felt when first she gazed upon her infant Jesus.

"Why do we celebrate Christmas?" asked Mrs. Waterman.

"Because Christ our Savior was born upon that day," promptly responded Elsie.

"More than two thousand years ago," began Mrs. Waterman, "Melchior, Gaspar, and Balthazar, three very wise men, had heard that Jesus was to be born in Bethlehem of Judea. Melchior was a Greek, Gaspar was a Hindu, and Balthazar was an Egyptian. They lived very far apart, but each was told in a dream that he should see the Savior. Their hearts were filled with joy and thanksgiving, for they had never thought to have the privilege of gazing upon their Savior in person. The Spirit of God guided each one to a common meeting place: from there they were told to follow a star which was set in the heavens to guide them.

"Without doubt or misgiving they followed the star until it stopped over a stable in the little town of Bethlehem. 'This must be the place; we will enter,' said they. Trembling with hope and fear they entered, and there they saw the baby Jesus, sleeping in its mother's arms.

"The wise men knelt down and worshiped Jesus. Then they laid at his feet costly presents of frankincense, myrrh, incense, gold and precious jewels. It was then that Santa Claus was born. Santa Claus is the Spirit of Thankfulness that finds expression in gifts, and it will live so long as Christ shall reign upon earth and fill the hearts of men and women with His goodness and love."

"Does he always come to good little girls and good little boys?" asked Elsie, after she had thought awhile over the story.

"Always," answered Mrs. Waterman, slowly.

"Haven't I been a good little girl, little mother?" said Elsie wistfully.

"No little girl could have been better, my Lady," replied the mother, and again a pained expression crept into her face.

"I hope Santa will bring me the doll with the pretty brown face and Indian hair that I asked him for in my letter." Then a happy look came to Elsie's eyes. "Do you remember, little mother, you said if I prayed to the Good Man for anything I really wanted or needed, and believed that He would give me what I asked for, He'd do it?"

"I remember, little lady," answered Mrs. Waterman.

"Well," continued Elsie. "I want my papa very, very much, and I want a dolly, but mostly I want my papa, and I'm going to ask the Good Man to tell Santa to bring them to me tonight, so they will be here tomorrow for Christmas."

After stating her resolution, Elsie slipped down from her mother's knee and prepared for bed, filled with the happy anticipation that floods the hearts of children the world over on Christmas Eve.

For more than an hour Mrs. Waterman sat by the bedside of the slumbering child. It was the bitterest hour of her life. "If it wasn't for the little Lady, I wouldn't mind," she sobbed; "if it wasn't for little Lady, I wouldn't mind." Then she thought of the first happy months after she had married Fred. How happy and full of manly pride he had been when she confided the secret that she was soon to be a mother. She remembered how tenderly solicitous he was during the trying period that preceded Elsie's birth. Then the baby had come, and Fred seemed to have eyes and ears for nothing but the baby. Jealousy, like a serpent, had crept into her heart. She felt that she hated the baby and her husband also. Her mild manners and sweet disposition underwent a complete change. She became crabbed and cranky. Fred, at a loss to account for the sudden change in his wife, bore her continued ill-temper with patience and fortitude; but he continually lavished the affection of his generous heart more and more upon his daughter. The years dragged slowly by; but the strain they were undergoing told on each, until the year before it had reached the breaking point.

Mrs. Waterman remembered vividly that last Christmas. Fred had promised her a set of white furs. Just before Christmas he told her that his work had slackened and that she must wait until the New Year for her furs; in the meantime he had spent all his savings for Elsie's Christmas. How mean and selfish she had thought him then! They quarreled, and she had told him to go; angry at her injustice, he had taken her at her word and left.

For weeks after her father had gone, Elsie had refused to be comforted. Mrs. Waterman was forced to tell Elsie the one and only falsehood she had ever told her, that her father was away on business and would be back as soon as possible. It was during the following weeks and months of loneliness that Mrs. Waterman had learned to love her daughter. She saw herself as she had been, a narrow-minded, selfish woman. "If Fred would only return," she murmured, "how different I would be!"

Mrs. Waterman had been put to her wits' end to provide for the little household. Not having been schooled in the art of economizing, her expenses were always more than her income. She had been forced to the humiliating expedient of pawning her jewelry; then her clothes, and lastly the furniture. Now it was Christmas Eve, and not a cent to buy Elsie a present. How could she face the disappointed look of Elsie's bright eyes when they opened in the morning and

found that Santa had passed her by? As the thought took full possession of Mrs. Waterman's mind, she fell upon her knees and sobbed
in anguish. Then she prayed, "O God, send my husband to me!
Give my baby her Christmas!"

A loud knock at the door brought Mrs. Waterman to her feet in
quick alarm. She pressed her hand to her heart to still its tumultuous
beating. The knock was repeated, this time louder, as if the knocker
were growing impatient. Not knowing what to expect, she opened
the door, and gazed in the face of a special delivery boy.

"Is this 332 X. Street?" the boy asked.

"It is," Mrs. Waterman replied.

"A package for you." And the boy shoved a large box into her
hands.

"There must be some mistake," began Mrs. Waterman, but the
boy was walking rapidly away, whistling with pleasure that his last
errand had been completed.

Trembling with excitement, Mrs. Waterman proceeded to undo
the package. The first thing that greeted her eyes was a beautiful
brown-skin doll. "Oh, how happy Lady will be!" she exclaimed.
Smiling through her tears at the thought of Elsie's happiness, she
proceeded to remove a layer of tissue paper, and there disclosed to
her view was a set of handsome snow-white furs. Laughing and crying by turns, she fell upon her knees and buried her face in its soft
fleece. "Fred has not forgotten us, little Lady," she whispered.

While Mrs. Waterman was yet upon her knees, the familiar
melody of a whistler was borne to her ears. Only one person had
ever whistled that little melody; could it be him, she wondered?
Fred had always repeated the little strain at the next corner, so she
would always be sure it was him. Now she waited breathlessly for the

repetition; her nerves were strained to their utmost tension. Then, just as she was sure it would not recur, clear and sweet, the little melody broke upon the midnight air. Every doubt was dispelled. It was Fred! She arose from her knees. Her trembling knees threatened to give way and leave her sprawled upon the floor; she grasped the foot of the bed for support; the blood had receded from her face, leaving it pale and cold.

Now she could hear his footfalls upon the gravel walk. She had always loved to hear his firm and regular tread. As the footfalls drew nearer the door, they hesitated, as if the walker were in doubt whether to proceed or retire. Mrs. Waterman felt that she would faint. The steps drew nearer; now they were crossing the little porch; they hesitated at the door a moment; then came a knock. Even in this Mrs. Waterman recognized her husband's thoughtfulness; he was afraid to enter without knocking, as was his custom, not knowing what effect his sudden appearance might have upon his family. Mrs. Waterman heard the knock and tried to answer; only an inarticulate sound issued from her dry and parched throat. Impatient at not receiving an answer to his knock and fearful that something might be wrong, Fred opened the door, stepped across the threshold and stood face to face with his wife.

They seemed incapable of speech. Mrs. Waterman swayed slightly, but recovered herself with an effort. The husband was the first to speak.

"Virgie," he said, and his voice sounded strange and unnatural; "Virgie," he repeated, "I couldn't stay away another minute; 'deed I couldn't."

Mrs. Waterman wondered if she would ever regain her power of speech.

"It didn't seem right," continued Fred, "to be away from you and Lady on Christmas day."

Mrs. Waterman stood like a graven image, with eyes riveted upon her husband's face.

"I—I—thought—you might—you might be a little glad to see me," faltered the man. There was a sound of tears in his voice as he continued: "If—if—you'll just let me spend Christmas with you—and Lady—I'll promise to go away and—and—never see you again."

This momentary weakness in the man touched the woman as nothing else could have done. All the love of a good and true woman shone in her eyes and suffused her face. With quivering lips she cried: "O Fred! Fred! How could you!" She took one step toward her husband, faltered, swayed; at one stride the husband had her in his arms, crushed to his breast; her arms were about his neck. "I've wanted you so much, Freddie boy, so very, very much," she sobbed.

Manly tears were running down the husband's cheeks. "It was all my fault, girlie," he said.

"No! No!" she cried, "the fault was mine. I was little, mean, and jealous; and oh! the shame of it. I was jealous of my own daughter."

"Hush, Virgie," commanded the husband. "I should have been more of a man. My love and sympathy should have made me understand. I was conceited; you wounded my pride and vanity, and I left you—left my wife and baby to the mercy of strangers. Virgie," he pleaded, "can you ever forgive me?"

"There is nothing to forgive, Freddie boy," she answered; "we have both been foolish. I was as guilty as you; but what does it matter, since we are together again."

Roused by the sound of voices, Elsie sat up in bed. "Little

mother, has papa come?" she asked, drowsily. The father loosened his wife's arms from about his neck, bounded to the bedside and gathered the little girl into his arms, where she nestled affectionately. "I knowed Santa would bring you to me and little mother," she murmured.

"He didn't forget to send the dolly," said the mother, as she held it before Elsie's wondering eyes.

Just then the clock in the tower began to strike the midnight hour. Immediately the Trinity chimes began to ring out the melody of that wonderful hymn, "All hail the power of Jesus' name." While the beautiful tones echoed and vibrated upon the midnight air, the three stood with arms entwined about each other. After the last sweet strain had whispered itself away into the silence of the winter night, the father said, "It is Christmas now, little Lady,"

"God is very good," murmured the mother.

"So is Santa Claus," whispered Elsie.

GENERAL WASHINGTON:
A CHRISTMAS STORY

Pauline Elizabeth Hopkins

Widely known as a writer, editor, playwright, singer, and actress, Pauline Elizabeth Hopkins was born in Portland, Maine, in 1859. As the great grandniece of poet James Whitfield, a descendant of Nathaniel and Thomas Paul, founder of the Baptist churches in Boston, Hopkins was steeped in black middle-class life and culture. However, her exposure and intimate knowledge of the folklore, lifestyles, and speech patterns of Southern black migrants, many of whom belonged to the Baptist and Methodist churches in Boston, provided her with ample materials for her novels, short stories, plays, and nonfictional works. Hopkins, a pioneering writer, was exceptionally gifted and prolific. Her familiarity with black accomplishments, racial movements, and race-related issues is manifested in her fiction, drama, and essays.

As the literary editor of the *Colored American Magazine*, one of the first African American journals to offer black writers an open forum for expression, Hopkins became known as one of its major contributors. The majority of her short stories, biographical sketches of black historical figures, and serialized novels appeared in the magazine between 1900 and mid-1904. A keen observer of black life and culture, she believed that black writers must use fiction to tell the story of African American life and history.

"General Washington: A Christmas Story" and six other short stories were published in the *Colored American Magazine*. Hopkins's fiction, particularly her novels, tended to focus on the black Southern elite and upper middle class, but many of her short stories are centered on the life of the working class. "General Washington," published in the December 1900 issue of the *Colored American Magazine*, is rich in black vernacular speech, folklore, and culture. It includes a number of themes related to the African American condition at the turn of the twentieth century. Set in Washington, DC, the story features social commentary to focus on issues related to racism, religion, the survival of the urban black poor, spousal abuse, child neglect and abuse, crime, and even miscegenation. This is all accomplished through an exploration of the exploits of "General Washington."

The central characters of this story are "General Washington," Fairy, and Senator Tallman. "General Washington," also known as Buster, is a formally uneducated but street smart ten-year-old orphan, who is hustling for survival among the food and produce stalls at the Washington Market where "his specialty was selling chitlins." He is a "knight of the pavement," who dances on the street and in saloons for pay; a leader of a gang of street urchins; a survivor who "lived in the very shady atmosphere of Murderer's Bay," in a box turned on end and filled with straw. Fairy, the granddaughter of Senator Tallman, meets General Washington while shopping with her nanny. Following a brief observation of General Washington unscrupulously selling chitterlings to buyers in the market, Fairy introduces herself and invites him to come to her home on Christmas morning to learn about God and atone for his un-Christian ways. Senator Tallman is a former slave owner and Confederate army veteran who regains his senatorial seat after Reconstruction ends. He is an embittered man who professes his hatred for "Negroes" and opposes any black advancement.

Hopkins skillfully used naming as a device to delineate the characters. Thus, "General," or "Buster," is a leader. "General Washington ranked first among the knights of the pavement," Hopkins writes. Fairy represents an imaginary, tiny, graceful figure whom the General had learned about in his short stay at school. When he meets the blue-eyed, well-dressed white Fairy, he is awestruck. Hopkins describes Tallman as a larger-than-life, pompous racist who is preparing to deliver a speech before the Senate that would "bury the blacks too deep for resurrection and settle the Negro question forever." Tallman, the fictional senator, was in some ways a parody of the real-life Senator Benjamin Tillman, who gained great visibility during the 1870s as an activist in the movement to overthrow the Republican-dominated Reconstruction government in South Carolina. A rabid racist, he was elected governor of South Carolina in 1890 and by 1894 was in the US Senate. Tillman was widely known for his virulently bigoted comments and conscientious efforts to pass the South Carolina Constitution of 1895, which disfranchised African American men. Through the characters of the General and Senator Tallman, Hopkins demonstrates that Christmas is a time of rebirth, salvation, and redemption in Christ.

Hopkins also refers to a particular cultural practice that is not well known today: the Juba, a popular slave dance based on an African step called Giouba, an elaborate jig. Like his forebears,

General Washington and other dancers engaged in competitions to determine who was the most skillful and agile dancer, and who could dance the best and the longest.

General Washington:
A Christmas Story

I.

General Washington did any odd jobs he could find around the Washington market, but his specialty was selling chitlins.

General Washington lived in the very shady atmosphere of Murderer's Bay in the capital city. All that he could remember of father or mother in his ten years of miserable babyhood was that they were frequently absent from the little shanty where they were supposed to live, generally after a protracted spell of drunkenness and bloody quarrels when the police were forced to interfere for the peace of the community. During these absences, the child would drift from one squalid home to another wherever a woman—God save the mark!—would take pity upon the poor waif and throw him a few scraps of food for his starved stomach, or a rag of a shawl, apron or skirt, in winter, to wrap about his attenuated little body.

One night the General's daddy being on a short vacation in the city, came home to supper; and because there was no supper to eat, he occupied himself in beating his wife. After that time, when the officers took him, the General's daddy never returned to his home. The General's mammy? Oh, she died!

General Washington's resources developed rapidly after this.

Said resources consisted of a pair of nimble feet for dancing the hoe-down, shuffles intricate and dazzling, and the Juba; a strong pair of lungs, a wardrobe limited to a pair of pants originally made for a man, and tied about the ankles with strings, a shirt with one gallows, a vast amount of "brass," and a very, very small amount of nickel. His education was practical; "Ef a corn-dodger costs two cents, an' a fellar hain't got de two cents, how's he gwine ter git de corn-dodger?"

General Washington ranked first among the knights of the pavement. He could shout louder and hit harder than any among them; that was the reason they called him "Buster" and "the General." The General could swear, too; I am sorry to admit it, but the truth must be told.

He uttered an oath when he caught a crowd of small white aristocrats tormenting a kitten. The General landed among them in quick time and commenced knocking heads at a lively rate. Presently he was master of the situation, and marched away triumphantly with the kitten in his arms, followed by stones and other missiles which whirled about him through space from behind the safe shelter of back yards and street corners.

The General took the kitten home. Home was a dry-goods box turned on end and filled with straw for winter. The General was as happy as a lord in summer, but the winter was a trial. The last winter had been a hard one, and Buster called a meeting of the leading members of the gang to consider the advisability of moving farther south for the hard weather.

"'Pears lak to me, fellers, Wash'nton's heap colder'n it uster be, an' I'se mighty onscruplus 'bout stoppin' hyar."

"Business am mighty peart," said Teenie, the smallest member of the gang, "s'pose we put off menderin' tell after Chris'mas; Jeemes Henry, fellers, it hain't no Chris'mas fer me outside ob Wash'nton."

"Dat's so, Teenie," came from various members as they sat on the curbing playing an interesting game of craps.

"Den hyar we is tell after Chris'mas, fellers; then dis sonny's gwine ter move, sho, hyar me?"

"De gang's wid yer, Buster; move it is."

It was about a week before Chris'mas, and the weather had been unusually severe.

Probably because misery loves company—nothing could be more miserable than his cat—Buster grew very fond of Tommy. He would cuddle him in his arms every night and listen to his soft purring while he confided all his own hopes and fears to the willing ears of his four-footed companion, occasionally pulling his ribs if he showed any signs of sleepiness.

But one night poor Tommy froze to death. Buster didn't— more's the wonder—only his ears and his two big toes. Poor Tommy was thrown off the dock into the Potomac the next morning, while a stream of salt water trickled down his master's dirty face, making visible, for the first time in a year, the yellow hue of his complexion. After that the General hated all flesh and grew morose and cynical.

Just about a week before Tommy's death, Buster met the fairy. Once, before his mammy died, in a spasm of reform she had forced him to go to school, against his better judgment, promising the teacher to go up and "wallop" the General every day if he thought Buster needed it. This gracious offer was declined with thanks. At the end of the week the General left school for his own good and the good of the school. But in that week he learned something about fairies; and so, after she threw him the pinks [flowers] that she carried in her hand, he called her to himself "the fairy."

Being Christmas week, the General was pretty busy. It was a

great sight to see the crowds of people coming and going all day long about the busy market; wagon loads of men, women and children, some carts drawn by horses, but more by mules. Some of the people well-dressed, some scantily clad, but all intent on getting enjoyment out of this their leisure season. This was the season for selling crops and settling the year's account. The store-keepers, too, had prepared their most tempting wares, and the thoroughfares were crowded.

"I 'clare to de Lord, I'se done busted my ol' man, shure," said one woman to another as they paused to exchange greetings outside a store door.

"N'em min'," returned the other, "he'll wurk fer mo'. Dis is Chris'mas, honey."

"To be sure," answered the first speaker, with a flounce of her ample skirts.

Meanwhile her husband pondered the advisability of purchasing [a] mule, feeling in his pockets for the price demanded, but finding them nearly empty. The money had been spent on the annual festival.

"Ole mule, I want yer mighty bad, but you'll have to slide dis time; it's Chris'mas, mule."

The wise old mule actually seemed to laugh as he whisked his tail against his bony sides and steadied himself on his three sound legs.

The vendors were very busy, and their cries were wonderful for ingenuity of invention to attract trade:

"Hello, dar, in de cellar, I'se got fresh aggs fer de'casion; now's year time fer agg-nogg wid new aggs in it."

There were the stalls, too, kept by venerable aunties and filled with specimens of old-time southern cheer: Coon, corn-pone, possum fat and hominy; there were piles of gingerbread and boiled chestnuts, heaps of walnuts and roasting apples. There were great barrels of cider, not to speak of something stronger. There were terrapin and the persimmon and the chinquapin in close proximity to the succulent viands—shine and spare-rib, sausage and crackling, savory souvenirs of the fine art of hog-killing. And everywhere were faces of dusky hue; Washington's great Negro population bubbled over in every direction.

The General was peddling chitlins. He had a tub upon his head and was singing in his strong childish tones:

> Here's yer chitlins, fresh an' sweet.
> Young hog's chitlins hard to beat,
> Methodis chitlins, jes' been biled,
> Right fresh chitlins, dey ain't spiled,
> Baptis' chitlins by de pound,
> As nice chitlins as ever was foun.

"Hyar, boy, duz yer mean ter say dey is real Baptis' chitlins, sho nuff?"

"Yas, mum."

"How duz you make dat out?"

"De hog raised by Mr. Robberson, a hard-shell Baptis', mum."

"Well, lem-me have two poun's."

"Now," said a solid-looking man as General finished waiting on a crowd of women and men, "I want some o' de Methodes chitlins you's bin hollerin' 'bout."

"Hyar dey is, ser."

"Take 'em all out o' same tub?"

"Yas, ser. Only dair leetle mo' water on de Baptis' chitlins, an' dey's whiter."

"How you tell 'em?"

"Well, ser, two hog's chitlins in dis tub an one ob de hogs raised by Unc, Bemis, an' he's a Methodes,' ef dat don't make him a Methodes hog nuthin' will."

"Weigh me out four pounds, ser."

In an hour's time the General had sold out. Suddenly at his elbow he heard a voice:

"Boy, I want to talk to you."

The fairy stood beside him. She was a little girl about his own age, well wrapped in costly velvet and furs; her long, fair hair fell about her like an aureole of glory; a pair of gentle blue eyes set in a sweet, serious face glanced at him from beneath a jaunty hat with a long curling white feather that rested light as thistle-down upon the beautiful curly locks. The General could not move for gazing, and as his wonderment grew his mouth was extended in a grin that revealed the pearly whiteness of two rows of ivory.

"Boy, shake hands."

The General did not move; how could he?

"Don't you hear me?" asked the fairy, imperiously:

"Yas'm," replied the General meekly. "'Deed, missy, I'se 'tirely too dirty to tech dem clos o' yourn."

Nevertheless he put forth timidly and slowly a small paw begrimed with the dirt of the street. He looked at the hand and then at her; she looked at the hand and then at him. Then their eyes meeting, they laughed the sweet laugh of the free-masonry of childhood.

"I'll excuse you this time, boy," said the fairy, graciously, "but you must remember that I wish you to wash your face and hands when you are to talk with me; and," she added, as though inspired by an afterthought, "it would be well for you to keep them clean at other times, too."

"Yas'm," replied the General.

"What's your name, boy?"

"Gen'r'l Wash'nton," answered Buster, standing at attention as he had seen the police do in the court-room.

"Well, General, don't you know you've told a story about the chitlins you've just sold?"

"Tol' er story?" queried the General with a knowing look. "Course I got to sell my chitlins ahead ob de oder fellars, or lose my trade."

"Don't you know it's wicked to tell stories?"

"How come so?" asked the General, twisting his bare toes about in his rubbers, and feeling very uncomfortable.

"Because, God says we musn't."

"Who's he?"

The fairy gasped in astonishment. "Don't you know who God is?"

"No'pe; never seed him. Do he live in Wash'nton?"

"Why, God is your Heavenly Father, and Christ was His son. He was born on Christmas Day a long time ago. When He grew a man, wicked men nailed Him to the cross and killed Him. Then He went to heaven, and we'll all live with Him some day if we are good before we die. O I love Him; and you must love Him, too, General."

"Now look hyar, missy, you kayn't make this chile b'lieve nufin lak dat."

The fairy went a step nearer the boy in her eagerness:

"It's true; just as true as you live."

"Whar'd you say He lived?"

"In heaven," replied the child, softly.

"What kin' o' place is heaven?"

"Oh, beautiful!"

The General stared at the fairy. He worked his toes faster and faster.

"Say, kin yer hab plenty to eat up dar?"

"O, yes; you'll never be hungry there."

"An' a fire, an' clos?" he queried in suppressed, excited tones.

"Yes; it's all love and plenty when we get to heaven, if we are good here."

"Well, missy, dat's a pow'ful good story, but I'm blamed ef I b'lieve it." The General forgot his politeness in his excitement.

"An' ef it's true, tain't only fer white fo'ks; you won't fin' nary nigger dar."

"But you will; and all I've told you is true. Promise me to come to my house on Christmas morning and see my mother. She'll help you, and she will teach you more about God. Will you come? she asked eagerly, naming a street and number in the most aristocratic quarter of Washington. "Ask for Fairy, that's me. Say quick; here is my nurse."

The General promised.

"Law, Miss Fairy, honey; come right hyar. I'll tell yer mamma how you's done run 'way from me to talk to dis dirty little monkey. Pickin' up sech trash fer ter talk to."

The General stood in a trance of happiness. He did not mind the slurring remarks of the nurse, and refrained from throwing a brick at the buxom lady, which was a sacrifice on his part. All he saw was the glint of golden curls in the winter sunshine, and the tiny hand waving him good-bye.

"Ah' her name is Fairy! Jes' ter think how I hit it all by my lonesome."

Many times that week the General thought and puzzled over Fairy's words. Then he would sigh:

"Heaven's where God lives. Plenty to eat, warm fire all de time in winter; plenty o' clos,' too, but I'se got to be good. 'Spose dat means keepin' my face an' hand's clean an' stop swearing' an' lyin.' It kayn't be did."

The gang wondered what had come over Buster.

II.

The day before Christmas dawned clear and cold. There was snow on the ground. Trade was good, and the General, mindful of the visit next day, had bought a pair of second-hand shoes and a new calico shirt.

"Git onter de dude!" sang one of the gang as he emerged from the privacy of the dry-goods box early Christmas Eve.

The General was a dancer and no mistake. Down at Dutch Dan's place they kept the old-time Southern Christmas moving along in hot time until the dawn of Christmas Day stole softly through the murky atmosphere. Dutch Dan's was the meeting place of the worst characters, white and black, in the capital city. From that vile den issued the twin spirits murder and rapine as the early winter shadows fell; there the criminal entered in the early dawn and was lost to the accusing eye of justice. There was a dance at Dutch Dan's Christmas Eve, and the General was sent for to help amuse the company.

The shed-like room was lighted by oil lamps and flaring pine torches. The center of the apartment was reserved for dancing. At one end the inevitable bar stretched its yawning mouth like a monster awaiting his victims. A long wooden table was built against one side of the room, where the game could be played to suit the taste of the most expert devotee of the fickle goddess.

The room was well filled, early as it was, and the General's entrance was the signal for a shout of welcome. Old Unc' Jasper was tuning his fiddle and blind Remus was drawing sweet chords from an old banjo. They glided softly into the music of the Mobile shuffle. The General began to dance. He was master of the accomplishment. The pigeon-wing, the old buck, the hoe-down and the Juba followed each other in rapid succession. The crowd shouted and cheered and joined in the sport. There was hand-clapping and a rhythmic accompaniment of patting the knees and stamping the feet. The General danced faster and faster:

> Juba up and juba down,
> Juba all aroun' de town;
> Can't you hyar de juba pat? Juba!

sang the crowd. The General gave fresh graces and new embellishments. Occasionally he added to the interest by yelling, "Ain't dis fin'e!" "Oh, my!" "Now I'm gittin' loose!" "Hol' me, hol' me!"

The crowd went wild with delight.

The child danced until he fell exhausted to the floor. Someone in the crowd "passed the hat." When all had been waited upon the barkeeper counted up the receipts and divided fair—half to the house and half to the dancer. The fun went on, and the room grew more crowded. General Wash'nton crept under the table and curled himself up like a ball. He was lucky, he told himself sleepily, to have so warm a berth that cold night; and then his heart glowed as he thought of the morrow and Fairy, and wondered if what she had said were true. Heaven must be a fine place if it could beat the floor under the table for comfort and warmth. He slept. The fiddle creaked, the dancers shuffled. Rum went down their throats and wits were befogged. Suddenly the General was wide awake with a start. What was that?

"The family are all away to-night at a dance, and the servants gone home. There's no one there but an old man and a kid. We can be well out of the way before the alarm is given. 'Leven sharp, Doc. And, look here, what's the number agin?"

Buster knew in a moment that mischief was brewing, and he turned over softly on his side, listening mechanically to catch the reply. It came. Buster sat up. He was wide awake then. They had given the street and number where Fairy's home was situated.

III.

Senator Tallman was from Maryland. He had owned slaves, fought in the Civil War on the Confederate side, and at its end had been returned to a seat in Congress after Reconstruction, with feelings of deeply rooted hatred for the Negro. He openly declared his purpose to oppose their progress in every possible way. His favorite argument was disbelief in God's handiwork as shown in the Negro.

"You argue, suh, that God made 'em, I have my doubts, suh, God made man in His own image, suh, and that being the case, suh, it is clear that he had no hand in creating niggers. A nigger, suh, is the image of nothing but the devil." He also declared in his imperious, haughty, Southern way; "The South is in the saddle, suh, and she will never submit to the degradation of Negro domination; never suh."

The Senator was a picture of honored age and solid comfort seated in his velvet armchair before the fire of blazing logs in his warm, well-lighted study. His lounging coat was thrown open, revealing its soft silken lining, his feet were thrust into gayly embroidered fur-lined slippers. Upon the baize covered table beside him a silver salver sat holding a decanter, glasses and fragrant mint, for the Senator loved the beguiling sweetness of a mint julep at bedtime. He was writing a speech which in his opinion would bury the blacks too deep for resurrection and settle the Negro question forever. Just now he was idle; the evening paper was folded across his knees; a smile was on his face. He was alone in the grand mansion, for the festivities of the season had begun and the family were gone to enjoy a merry-making at the house of a friend. There was a picture in his mind of Christmas in his old Maryland home in the good old days "befo' de wah," the great ball-room where giggling girls and matrons fair glided in the stately minuet. It was in such a gathering he had met his wife, the beautiful Kate Channing. Ah, the happy time of youth and love! The house was very still; how loud the ticking of the clock sounded. Just then a voice spoke beside his chair:

"Please, sah, I'se Gen'r'l Wash'nton."

The Senator bounded to his feet with an exclamation:

"Eh! Bless my soul, suh; where did you come from?"

"Ef yer please, boss, froo de winder."

The Senator rubbed his eyes and stared hard at the extraordinary figure before him. The Gen'r'l closed the window and then walked up to the fire, warmed himself in front, then turned around and stood with his legs wide apart and his shrewd little gray eyes fixed upon the man before him.

The Senator was speechless for a moment; then he advanced upon the intruder with a roar warranted to make a six-foot man quake in his boots:

"Through the window, you black rascal! Well, I reckon you'll go out through the door, and that in quick time, you little thief."

"Please, boss, it hain't me; it's Jim the crook and de gang from Dutch Dan's."

"Eh!" said the Senator again.

"What's yer cronumter say now, boss? 'Leven is de time fer de perfahmance ter begin. I reckon'd I'd git hyar time nuff fer yer ter call de perlice."

"Boy, do you mean for me to understand that burglars are about to raid my house?" demanded the Senator, a light beginning to dawn upon him.

The General nodded his head:

"Dat's it, boss, ef by 'buglers' you mean Jim de crook and Dutch Dan." It was ten minutes of the hour by the Senator's watch. He went to the telephone, rang up the captain of the nearest station, and told him the situation. He took a revolver from a drawer of his desk and advanced toward the waiting figure before the fire.

"Come with me. Keep right straight ahead through that door; if you attempt to run I'll shoot you."

They walked through the silent house to the great entrance doors and there awaited the coming of the police. Silently the officers surrounded the house. Silently they crept up the stairs into the now darkened study. "Eleven" chimed the little silver clock on the mantel. There was the stealthy tread of feet a moment after, whispers, the flash of a dark lantern,—a rush by the officers and a stream of electricity flooded the room.

"It's the nigger did it!" shouted Jim the crook, followed instantly by the sharp crack of a revolver. General Washington felt a burning pain shoot through his breast as he fell unconscious to the floor. It was all over in a moment. The officers congratulated themselves on the capture they had made—a brace of daring criminals badly wanted by the courts.

When the General regained consciousness, he lay upon a soft, white bed in Senator Tallman's house. Christmas morning had dawned clear cold and sparkling; upon the air the joy-bells sounded sweet and strong: "Rejoice, your Lord is born." Faintly from the streets came the sound of merry voices: "Chris'mas gift, Chris'mas gift."

The child's eyes wandered aimlessly about the unfamiliar room as if seeking and questioning. They passed the Senator and Fairy, who sat beside him and rested on a copy of Titian's matchless Christ which hung over the mantel. A glorious stream of yellow sunshine fell upon the thorn-crowned Christ.

> God of Nazareth, see!
> Before a trembling soul
> Unfoldeth like a scroll
> Thy wondrous destiny!

The General struggled to a sitting position with arms outstretched, then fell back with a joyous, awesome cry:

"It's Him! It's Him!"

"O' General," sobbed Fairy, "don't you die, you're going to be happy all the rest of your life Grandpa says so."

"I was in time, little Missy; I tried mighty hard after I knowed whar' dem debbils was a-comin' to."

Fairy sobbed; the Senator wiped his eyeglasses and coughed. The General lay quite still a moment, then turned himself again on his pillow to gaze at the pictured Christ.

'I'm a-gittin' sleepy, missy, it's so warm an' comfurtable here. 'Pears lak I feel right happy sence Ise seed Him." The morning light grew brighter. The face of the Messiah looked down as it must have looked when He was transfigured on Tabor's heights. The ugly face of the child wore a strange, sweet beauty. The Senator bent over the quiet figure with a gesture of surprise.

The General had obeyed the call of One whom the winds and waves of stormy human life obey. Buster's Christmas Day was spent in heaven.

For some reason, Senator Tallman never made his great speech against the Negro.

THE AUTOBIOGRAPHY
OF A DOLLAR BILL

Lelia Plummer

"The Autobiography of a Dollar Bill" was published by the *Colored American Magazine* in December 1904. Little is known about Lelia Plummer. Many of the early black newspapers and periodicals in which she published provided little or no biographical information.

The story is a mixture of allegory and fantasy that briefly describes the journey of "Mr. Dollar Bill." Written at the beginning of the twentieth century, following the Civil War, the end of Reconstruction, and the historic *Plessy v. Ferguson* Supreme Court decision, which sanctioned segregation, the story proposes a journey akin to the American slave experience, from the feelings of race memory, terror, landlessness, and claustrophobia during the Middle Passage to the severance of relations and relationships with the "ding, click" of the slave trade.

Utilizing Christmas as a vehicle and the dollar bill as a metaphor for the slave, Plummer examines the African American experience. The dollar bill, like the slave, was a commodity that was constantly being traded, thus each goes through a succession of owners and has a myriad of experiences. She explores the elements of bondage, status, self-definition, self-assertion, hope, and survival through

"Mr. Dollar Bill," as he tells his story to a street-smart, homeless urchin named Jackie, who has become the bill's most recent owner on a cold wintry Christmas Eve. As a benevolent owner, Jackie wants to keep his valuable possession, but circumstances dictate that this is impossible, and he intends to treat himself to "pleasures" on Christmas Day. This valuable property must be passed on to a new owner in order for Jackie to improve his wretched condition.

Perhaps Plummer read and used as a model *The Interesting Narrative of the Life of Olaudah Equiano, or Gustavus Vassa, the African*. In his revealing account of enslavement, Vassa tells of his African heritage, being kidnapped, being sold to slave traders, his experience in the Middle Passage, life on the American plantation, and his acculturation in America. Plummer's use of "Mr. Dollar Bill," in the role of a griot, suggests how the oral tradition functioned to acculturate Africans to American slavery and to preserve African heritage among the enslaved. "Mr. Dollar Bill" tells of the experience of being surrounded by "heaps of others just like me"; being placed in a "great big, hollow, cold place"; being "snatched" and "plunged into darkness"; and of conversing with elders who told him of their varied experiences in a bewildering world of uncertainty and confinement. And, like Vassa, "Mr. Dollar Bill" had found his English sea captain in the likes of Jackie.

The Autobiography of a Dollar Bill

It was Christmas Eve. The earth was covered with a white fluffy mantle. The snow gleamed brightly on the branches of the frozen trees, where a few brown little sparrows chirped cheerfully. The houses were covered with snow, and every few minutes might be heard the merry ringing of sleigh bells.

"Hullo" said ragged Jackie. "This is the kind of a Christmas for me; none o' yur mild dripping Christmases is this, but a good old-timer." The shivering little urchin addressed replied, that "As for them that has fires, a snowy Christmas [is] all right," but he was cold. "Anyway," he concluded, "it ain't Christmas, it's only Christmas Eve, and I want to know what you're going to do when Christmas really comes?"

"Well," said Jackie, "just now I'm goin' to sell my papers and earn some stray cash; then I'm goin' to that little corner of the bridge and cuddle down, and to-morrer, I'll treat myself with my cash." So away he trudged, crying "Paper here, sir, DAILY NEWS, and special Christmas numbers!" But few seemed to hear the little one, so intent were all upon their Christmas shopping. But suddenly in crossing the street, Jackie lost his footing and nearly fell under the heels of a dashing pair of horses, which were drawing an elegant equipage up the street. The coachman sprang down and kindly raised the little arab in his arms. "Why youngster, you want to be careful! Are you hurt?" Then the carriage door opened and a kind face looked out upon little Jackie, who was endeavoring to wrest himself from the coachman's arms.

"Are you hurt, little fellow?" a sweet voice asked. "No um" responded the blushing Jackie. Then seeing his rags, a kind hand drew forth some money from a bag and slipped it into the newsboy's hand. The coachman took his seat, and in a moment the carriage had passed on.

Jackie gazed upon the money in his dirty little hand, scarcely able to believe his own eyes. Yes, in that brown little palm lay a clear, crisp one dollar bill. Jackie hugged himself with delight, and clasping his dollar closely, danced off to resume his efforts to sell his papers. But people did not bother with Jackie any more that day, and when night came he had not sold one paper. Nevertheless his heart felt very light and he was happy. Many, many times during the day he had stolen a glance at the crisp little bill; and now when the bright and beautiful lights began to appear in the city street, he rushed off to his little niche in the bridge where he was pleased to curl himself up for the night. "This here's better'n them old homes where you'r all tucked and cuddled like a girl" he used to say to his young companions. There he cuddled down, still hugging closely his precious dollar bill and thinking of the pleasures it would bring him Christmas day. Suddenly, to his surprise, he heard a squeaking little voice call "Jackie, say Jackie!" Jackie rubbed his eyes and looked around. He saw no one. Suddenly it came again, and this time Jackie did not look for it, but said, "All right, here I am; what do you want anyway?"

"See here, Jackie," the voice continued, "I'm Mr. Dollar Bill and I want to tell you all about me. But hug me up nice and tight, for night is cold." Jackie tightened his clutch upon the precious bill. "Now, I first sprang into this world of wonderful things in a place where I saw heaps of others just like me. Oh my, there were so many of them that my eyes just ached! And there were round little men who were very bright looking but kept very humble before me, for they seemed to know that they were not half so good or valuable as I.

"Then there were some little silvery things, which we called, 'little dimes,' and I believe there were more of them than any of us could ever imagine. Well, I stayed in this a good while, until I got really tired; at last somebody far larger and better clothed than you, Jackie, took me and put me in a great big, hollow, cold place. If I had been alone I would not have liked it at all, but there were lots of others just like me, only none of the shining things were there. I asked some of the more important men what it meant and they said 'Little ones were to be seen and not heard' and that I must live and learn. But I was not there long, for a great broad hand came and hauled me out. I felt myself being whirled through the air for a few moments, and then I was suddenly plunged into utter darkness. Ah Jackie! That was a black moment for me. I could not tell where I was. For a long while I felt as if I were moving. Then suddenly, I was whisked out again and put into a little, wee box and felt myself scudding along at a terrific rate. I wondered where I was going. I was snatched from there just as suddenly, but before I was again plunged into darkness, I caught a gleam of bright and pretty things and a great moving mass of people. Jackie, where was I?"

"Oh I guess somebody went to do some Christmas shopping as they call it, with you and took you into one of those beautiful stores."

"Very good" replied the bill complacently. "You're not a bad little chap for your age, Jackie, not at all. Well, to proceed with my tale, I met there an old friend, Jackie. Yes, my boy, and old friend, for I myself have had so many travels that I am beginning to feel old, though I look so bright and new. The last time I had seen him was when we lay in a great box together. He recognized me instantly and I began to talk to him. 'Hullo, old fellow?' I said, 'Here we are again. Now where have you been?' Then I noticed that beside him lay a very old and tattered gentleman, at whom I was inclined to turn up my nose, but bless me, Jackie, my friend seemed more inclined to notice the old one than he did me, the bright, the new and pretty. Just then came a ring and a click and my friend was gone.

"Then the old tattered fellow looked at me seriously and soberly for a few minutes, and began, 'An old fellow like myself, youngster, is really more valuable than a young one, like you. Oh! young ignorance, if you only knew the many and varied tales I could tell! Ha ha! Youngster, you look as if you thought you knew something.' Then I [blushed] and looked down, for do you know, Jackie, I didn't just like the way the fellow was talking. But he kept on. 'Why, green one, I have travelled across rough waters, over green fields. I have been in the homes of the rich, where there were many, many more like myself, and I have been in the homes of the poor, where there were none like myself. Little one, I have been where all was innocence and purity, and likewise where all was crime. Yes I have been snatched from wallets by crime-stained hands and been in the pockets of noted criminals. What phase of life have I not seen? I have been the poor man's joy, the miser's hoard, and until I fall in pieces, I shall continue to travel these rounds.' Ding, click! My acquaintance was gone.

"There were lots of other bills there, who, I do not doubt, were worthy of my notice, but really, Jackie, that last wonderful fellow had scarcely gone, when rude hands snatched me, sped me through space, and once more consigned me to gloom. But I did not mind the darkness so much this time, for I reflected upon the old one's story and hoped that I might live to be the ragged, worn old fellow he was. You see so much more of life, Jackie. While I studied and thought, I could hear sweet voices speaking and suddenly a kindlier and gentler hand gave me into your keeping. Some way or other I took a fancy to you directly. You seemed to treat a fellow as if he had some feeling and you had some consideration for it. I really like you, Jackie, and when Christmas morning comes and I am leaving you, for I suppose I must, do not grieve for I shall always be on the watch for you again."

"Oh no, you shall never go," cried Jackie with energy. He gave a start and sprang to his feet. It was early, early in the blessed Christmas morning and already the bells were chiming the birth of the Babe at Bethlehem. How they rang in Jackie's ears and heart.

"What! Have I been dreaming all this? Not a bit of it! I heard that dollar just as plain as I hear these bells and I know that even if I part with my dear old bill, he'll be on the lookout for me and someday I'll have him again."

MIRAMA'S CHRISTMAS TEST

Timothy Thomas Fortune

Journalist, writer, and civil rights leader, T. Thomas Fortune was born to enslaved parents in Marianna, Florida, on October 3, 1856. After the Civil War, he briefly attended schools sponsored by the Freedmen's Bureau. In 1876, he attended Howard University, in Washington, DC, but did not graduate. While in Washington, Fortune worked for the *People's Advocate*, a black newspaper. He married Carrie C. Smiley, and they had five children, two of whom reached adulthood. In 1879, Fortune moved to New York, where he worked as a printer. Around 1880, he became part owner of a weekly tabloid, the *Rumor*, which in 1881 became the *Globe*, with Fortune as its editor. Following the failure of the *Globe*, he began publishing the *New York Freeman*, which in 1887 became the *New York Age*. For many years, the *Age* had a reputation as the leading black newspaper in America, primarily because of Fortune's editorials, which condemned racial discrimination and demanded full equality for black citizens. Fortune's militancy drew extensive criticism from the white press.

In spite of its successful outreach and reputation, the *Age* was not a financial success. Fortune supplemented his income by writing for other publications. In the 1890s, he wrote for the *New York Sun*

and *Boston Transcript*, and he sold his freelance writing to a
number of other newspapers. Fortune also published the book
Black and White: Land and Politics in the South (1884), as well
as articles and short stories that appeared in the *Age* and other
black newspapers.

In 1896, the *Indianapolis Freeman* published "Mirama's
Christmas Test," a story that reflects the concerns of educated black
women who wished to marry men of equal stature. It is set in Jason,
Florida, on Christmas Eve around 1895 in the home of Mirama
Young, an upper-class, educated black schoolteacher. Mirama is
the daughter and only child of a prosperous builder and contractor,
who had been allowed to hire out his time before the Civil War.
Like Frederick Douglass and a small number of "trusted" slaves,
Mirama's father had enjoyed a status between that of a slave and
a free person. As a trusted slave, he moved freely, "acting as a
free person," contracting his time and giving his master an agreed
upon percentage of his earnings. This experience provided him the
background and knowledge necessary to establish his own business
after the war.

Mirama is engaged to Alexander Simpson, a mathematician
and "somewhat of an architect," who is the principal at the school
where Mirama teaches. Simpson's father shared the views of many
former slaves, including Booker T. Washington, who believed
that one should acquire all the education he or she could, but that
one should also have a practical skill. The owner of a successful
carpentry business, Simpson taught his son the carpenter's trade.
His wish was that Alexander would acquire a college education
and become a master carpenter and builder. His death before

Alexander finished his college course, and the satisfaction of his business debts, left the family with minimal funds. Alexander could have saved the business and property, but he thought that, as an educated man, carpentry was beneath him. Essentially this was the issue that divided Mirama and Alexander and threatened to break up their engagement.

This story echoes a theme that becomes a much-debated issue in the African American community, and one that Carter G. Woodson immortalized in *The Miseducation of the Negro* (1933). Woodson argued that college-educated blacks had become immersed in a superficial reality, embracing empty values, and that instead of becoming educated, they were miseducated. Many college-educated blacks chose jobs in the professions, whether they were suited for them or not, because this gave them status and freed them from working with their hands. It did not matter that these jobs paid less and that they may not have offered opportunity for advancement. It is through the characters of Mirama Young and Alexander Simpson that Fortune conveys his concern about blacks who reflected these beliefs.

Fortune presents the reader with a positive model of an African American woman who has a well-defined race and gender consciousness. He characterizes Mirama as an intelligent, outspoken, independent female, "intensely devoted to her race and its best interests," who is not willing to settle for a man who does not share her values. This indicates that there was a cadre of educated black women who held high expectations for themselves and their race and who were not willing to compromise and accept men who did not meet their standards.

At the same time, Fortune reinforces the idea of love between black women and black men, who are striving to better themselves and their race.

Mirama's Christmas Test

I t was Christmas Eve, and there was but little frost in the air, but it was frosty enough to make people move along briskly, as they stirred about Jason, in the land of sunshine and flowers, of mocking birds and alligators, getting together "Christmas things" for the little ones, and for the big ones, also; for it is very true, as the poet has said: "We are but children of a larger growth." Some of the large ones are bigger children than the small ones.

This is just what Mirama Young thought, as she sat near Alexander Simpson, in the neat parlor of her own home, in the upper part of Jason, and watched the big logs in the fireplace blaze and hiss. Mirama Young was angry.

These two young people were up-to-date Afro-Americans, with positive views on most subjects and with good sized tempers with which to back them up. They both taught school. Mr. Simpson taught for a living, but had no sort of love for the work. It seemed to him more dignified to teach school than to follow the trade of a carpenter, the mastery of which he had acquired in his youth, and for which he had real aptitude. His supreme ambition was to be a lawyer, with political influence, and all that. He even dreamed that someday he might be commissioned by the President as Minister Resident and

Consul General near the court of Faraway, a soft snap much sought after by ambitious men of his race.

Mirama taught school because she liked it, and because she was intensely devoted to her race and its best interests. She had a good home, and had graduated from a famous seminary at the head of her class. Her father was a builder and contractor, one of the old timers who hired his time before the war and had been hiring the time of other people ever since. He was a practical old gentleman, and thought there was nothing too good for Mirama, his only child.

Mirama was engaged to be married to Alexander Simpson. They had reached an agreement on that point, but there were others necessary to the fulfillment of their mutual pledges upon which they were still as far apart as the North and the South. They were argumentative and dogmatic, were Mirama and Alexander, in their discussions. There was nothing of the spoilt child about Mirama, but for so small a woman, she had enough will force for three women. When she put her small foot down, Alexander Simpson could not make her take it up, although he weighed almost twice as much as she did. This was very painful to Mr. Alexander Simpson, who was entirely devoted to Mirama and twice as sentimental as she, and not half as studious in burning the midnight oil. Indeed, Mr. Alexander Simpson did not possess a literary head, although he thought that he did. Mirama had come out of school at the head of her class. Alexander had come out at the foot of his, and during the year that she had taught under him in the city school she had upheld the discipline and the dignity of the work at the school.

Mr. Alexander Simpson was a fine mathematician and somewhat of an architect. He had learned the carpenter's trade in his youth, and his father hoped that with a college education, he would become a master carpenter and builder. His father died just before Alexander finished his college course, and as he had a great many irons in the fire at the time of his death, there wasn't much left for Alexander and his mother when all the creditors were satisfied.

Now if Alexander had been a wise young man, he would have taken up his father's business where his father left off. If he had done so he could have saved much of his father's business and property. But Alexander Simpson was not going to bother with the carpentering business, not if Alexander knew himself. He did not think it a proper sort of business for a young man with a college education. Any sort of a common man could be a carpenter, he thought, but any sort of a common man could not be a lawyer.

And just here it was that Mirama Young and Alexander Simpson differed, and so radically that Mirama had put her little foot down and Mr. Alexander Simpson could not budge it. They had been fighting it over for the hundredth time, this Christmas Eve, and had reached a point where silence had fallen upon them like a wet blanket. Mirama was immovable; Alexander was stubborn.

"I have reached the conclusion that we had better break off our engagement, Mr. Simpson," said Mirama, gloomily, staring into the fire.

"But you can't back out now, Mirama. You have gone too far for that."

"Oh, yes I can!" snapped Mirama. "It is never too late to back out when you find that you have made a mistake."

"But have you made a mistake?"

"Certainly. That is the reason I think it best to break the engagement."

"What is the mistake?" asked Alexander, meekly.

"What is it? Why you are as stubborn as I am, and that I give away to you as much as you do to me."

"Now, Mirama, be reasonable. You know that you are as stubborn as I am, and that I give away to you as much as you do to me."

"That is just it," exclaimed Mirama. "Neither of us ever gives away. One of us must give away. You don't expect me to do it, do you?"

Alexander did not know how to answer this question, so evaded it by asking another: "You don't love me a bit, do you, now?"

"You know I do," [Mirama said] reproachfully; "but you are so stubborn."

"Now, what am I most stubborn in?" asked Alexander, soothingly.

"Everything!" said Mirama, with a sweep of her arm. "Everything! You would provoke a saint." [Taking a] long pause [she said], "Now, take this law scheme of yours."

"Don't!" said Alexander. "We can't agree on that."

"If we can't agree on that, we shall not be able to agree on anything, and we had better not get married, and I won't marry you. So there!" Mirama had put her little foot down. Alexander argued and coaxed, but he made no headway. He was in despair. Things had never reached this stage before, and a compromise of some sort must be reached.

"What do you want me to do?" asked the strong man, desperately.

"What do I want you to do?" asked Mirama indignantly. "I've told you a hundred times, I want you to give up the idea of reading law, and I want you to stop teaching school, and I want you to go with my father in the carpenter business. You will never succeed in the law, and you don't like school teaching, and you know all about carpentering. My father wants you to help him. He's getting old, and can't attend to all his business. And I am not going to marry you unless you do what I want you to do in this matter."

Alexander had studied the question from a thousand points of view and he had reached the conclusion that the law was the business in life he wanted to follow and that the carpentering business was not up to his idea of dignity. What did he get a college education for; just to be a carpenter? Not much. "You needn't say another word," said Mirama. "I will not budge an inch. The business that was good enough for your father and that is good enough for mine is good enough for you. You couldn't make enough money as a lawyer to support me, and you know it."

"O, I don't think I know anything of the sort," exclaimed Alexander.

"Perhaps you don't," [Mirama said] dryly; "but I do, and I am not going to try the experiment. We don't need to argue the question anymore."

Mr. Alexander Simpson did not argue the question any more. He put on his thinking cap and kept it on, in dead silence, for ten minutes. Then a big spasm of pain passed over his face, and Mr. Alexander Simpson, for the first time in their courtship, surrendered.

"I have been trying to get you to fix the marriage day for a year, now, if I do what you want will you fix the date?"

"Certainly," said Mirama. "I will fix the day any time you say after you write your resignation to the school board."

"That is your Christmas test," said Mirama Young.

Alexander took his fountain pen and securing a sheet of paper wrote his resignation to the school board, to take effect at the end of the holidays, and handed it to Mirama. She read it through carefully and said:

"We'll fix the date of the wedding."

"To-morrow, at 3 o'clock," said Alexander.

"O, that is a Christmas test!" exclaimed Mirama.

"Yes; Mirama's Christmas test," said Alexander Simpson.

A CHRISTMAS PARTY
THAT PREVENTED A SPLIT
IN THE CHURCH

Margaret Black

In 1916, John Murphy, the editor of the *Baltimore Afro-American*, described Margaret Black as a "writer and thinker of experience" and "an occasional writer of delightful short stories." Indeed, she was all of this and more. Although we do not know where or when she was born, she began her writing career in 1896 as the editor of the paper's "Women's Column." The initial column, which appears to have lasted for less than a year, reappeared in 1916 and enjoyed a run of at least three years. Published simultaneously with the column were Black's short stories. An outspoken feminist, she announced to her readers, "This column has its limits as well as its purposes. The editor allows us only a short space and being women, of course we must bow to the inevitable." In her writings, she addressed a number of issues that reflected the distinct consciousness of black women in the past, a worldview that was distinctive from those of black men and white women.

Black's "Women's Column," as well as her short stories, provides a unique opportunity to discover how black women viewed their society and how they strove to change it. Short stories, such as "A Christmas Party That Prevented a Split in the Church," provided a definition of black women's culture, specifically their values, practices, and institutions, and their ways of looking at the world common to a large number of black women who belonged to the church missionary societies in the nineteenth and twentieth centuries. Given the large numbers of working- and middle-class women who participated in these organizations, as well as the fact that they represented a key base of power for black women, we are able to observe black women's consciousness and culture from a unique vantage point.

"A Christmas Party That Prevented a Split in the Church," published in 1916, is a story about the shortage of "eligible" men available to black women for establishing families. Black has recorded the thoughts, words, deeds, and feelings of black church women as they struggled to give meaning and definition to their lives. At the center of this text is an African American and a female consciousness rarely seen at this early date. The story is set in the village of St. Michaels, which has a small black population and one black church that appears to be affiliated with the African Methodist Episcopal denomination (the Mite Missionary Society suggests this connection).

Black centers this story in the church, emphasizing the centrality of the institution in the lives of African Americans. The story focuses as well on who will marry the most eligible bachelor. The plot revolves around the activities of the Ladies Aid Society, which is actively engaged in preparing for the arrival of the Reverend Jonathan Steele, a twenty-five-year-old minister who is single. The society is made up primarily of the wives of the all-male board of trustees and board of stewards, and includes some of the most powerful women in the church.

Although black church women have been traditionally perceived as being subordinate and powerless in a male-dominated institution, Black creates narrative strategies that stress the power these women wielded through their organizations. In doing so, she effectively recovers their voices and their sense of autonomy. At the center of this text is the empowerment of black women.

A Christmas Party That Prevented a Split in the Church

Part I

G oodness," exclaimed Milly Brown. "All these things to move and dust, they're a sight and if I had my way, I'd get rid of some of them. No single man needs all this trash around, especially a minister."

"Always getting rid of something," said Sara Simpson, "I declare you are the limit; perhaps you'll want to be getting rid of your daughter Alice—now we are having a new minister and he a single man."

"I guess you are the one who'll be wanting the minister to marry them," laughed Milly. But Sara Simpson did not see the joke, you see Sara was past thirty—and did not like it mentioned—had a lovely home in town and everybody knew she was sore at Mrs. Jake Todd because Jake preferred her when she was Margaret Clayton instead of Sara Simpson—whose father was the leading lawyer in town and who gave his wife and daughter anything they wanted.

Sara was a pretty girl, but Margaret was much prettier and had such a sweet disposition that everybody loved her, even if she did have to wear cheap cotton dresses—and her hats and coats two winters and couldn't afford furs. But Sara snubbed poor Margaret every chance she got and poor Milly Brown also—because she was Margaret's friend.

Mrs. Milly Brown was a widow with only one daughter who lived beyond the town a lonely way and made her living by doing plain sewing.

You see there was only one church in the very small town—you or I would call it a village—which would surely have insulted the small population of St. Michaels because they felt themselves very important people and more especially now—as they were able to support a minister by themselves.

No more circuit riding minister for them. Since attaining the dignity of supporting a minister and having a parsonage rent free— they had organized a Mite Society for the grown people and a Helping Hand Society for the young folks and a Sunday Afternoon Literary Society, hence the self-satisfied feeling among them.

Their last pastor had been a married man with a large family, a wife and six children, and the poor man had so much trouble and such poor charges (which is the fate of a good many Methodist ministers) that he felt after he got to St. Michaels that he should take a rest, and he rested so well, and so long, that the people sent the Bishop word they did not want him back. So the good Bishop had now sent them not only a young man, but a single one, and St. Michaels folks were going out of their way to make things pleasant for the new minister.

He was very young and considered a genius, and as St. Michaels always gave the parsonage ready furnished and found the good parson coal and wood—they felt that since this was a young man they should go a step further and stock his pantry with all things needful and have him a good housekeeper, so they had installed old Aunt Eliza West as his housekeeper.

There had been a meeting of the Ladies' Aid Society, and a Committee for the pastor's arrival.

The Board of Trustees and Board of Stewards had also held meetings, but the Ladies' Aid had taken things in their hands and the men were well content to step aside and let them do the work—as most of their wives belonged to the Aid Society and those whose wives did not, thought it good policy to not object.

So there was just lots of help—because as Mrs. Orion Tucker remarked, "Wherever they had a married minister all the women stayed at home except a few old stand-bys who could always be depended on, but if he was a single man, every spinster and young girl and married woman in the town was in evidence to help, they had all they needed and more."

So they scrubbed floors—cleaned paints and windows—and swept and dusted and polished dishes and silver until it seemed as tho the things would surely come to life and cry out—enough! oh, enough! or melt into nothing.

At last everything was in readiness and St. Michaels was in a state of expectancy.

Only Brother Tucker and Sister Marion Ford had attended the conference at Greenville and neither of them could give a very clear account of what he looked like.

Brother Tucker said, "He was a pretty pert and spry looking youngster," and Sister Marion Ford said, "He was a handsome young chap—straight and tall as a young poplar and with the snappiest black eyes she'd ever seen—altogether quite 'stinguished looking."

"But," as Marie Phillips sarcastically remarked, "you can't depend on either one of these old folks, because everybody is 'pert' and spry to Brother Tucker, who walks and talks pretty slick and as for Sister Marion Ford—Oh pshaw! she can't see good anyway."

But "all's well that ends well"—and Rev. Jonathan Steele had arrived and was quite all both Brother Tucker and Sister Ford had described, and more, some of them thought. In plain words—"he came, he saw, he conquered" and after several months with the town folks—he was still "the new preacher"—at least he was as new as seven months steady wear in a small town could leave him. You see new silver does not tarnish very quickly and Rev. Steele was still untarnished. Of course he made mistakes—and this Thursday night at the meeting of the Ladies' Aid they were discussing the fact that the Rev. Mr. Steele did not or could not seem to grasp the fact that Mrs. John Taylor was the leader of the Ladies' Aid and a shining light in the church, and that Mrs. Orion Tucker was to be church treasurer for life and that the Trustees and Stewards' Boards were composed of life time members and also that Mrs. St. Anthony was the head deaconess of the church and as her husband had donated the ground on which the church stood and donated five thousand dollars towards the building fund, she must be consulted on all matters pertaining to the welfare of the church.

How was the Rev. Jonathan Steele, not a day over twenty-five and a young snipe just out of college, as Mrs. Tucker emphatically declared, to realize the importance of each separate man's and woman's work in his ever increasing congregation.

Although after seven months—if he really had failed to grasp these many cited facts—it was no fault of the members of St. Michaels' Church.

"Things seem to be moving along rather smoothly," remarked Mrs. Phillips—"I think the Reverend has commenced to appreciate his charge"—which remark was due to the fact that the Rev. Steele had lately congratulated Mrs. Phillips on her executive ability.

The ladies were lingering over the task of sorting out table linen and dishes after the yearly oyster supper for the benefit of the Stewards' Board.

"Yes," said Mrs. Phillips, "how our girls did work; they are coming into the church and working like soldiers, and are not near so thoughtless and silly as they used to be."

"Oh yes!" said Mrs. Tucker sarcastically. "It is really remarkable how they work. An unmarried minister can inspire so much enthusiasm among spinsters—and women with marriageable daughters."

"Well, I'm not making any unkind remarks," said Mrs. Phillips virtuously.

"Well," replied Mrs. Tucker—"neither am I, but I can't help noticing things when they happen right under your nose. I have eyes to see with and although we might not care to spread it broad cast, we can all see the difference between the treatment accorded Rev. Butler and that given Rev. Steele. You see Rev. Butler was an antiquated married man, while Rev. Steele is a very live young man. With Rev Butler we crawled along and the community hardly knew we existed, while now we are increasing by leaps and bounds—fairly flying."

"Well," said Mrs. Phillips, "it's natural isn't it. The young—"

"Of course it's natural," broke in Mrs. Tucker. "Life is just a succession of thrills anyway, and we all run after that we don't have. Didn't I run a little after my old man Orion, and didn't you run after Nathan?"

"No, I didn't" snapped Mrs. Phillips, "I never took one step out of my way for Nathan Phillips."

"Oh, well, you grabbed him mighty quick when he asked you—and that's what I'm thinking about these girls and old maids—any one of them could grab Rev. Steele mighty quick if he asks them."

A light laugh startled them and made them turn rather quickly—they had forgotten they were in church.

"I'm glad my girl lives such a distance from the church—that she can't take part in everything. Until she does her school work and helps me a little, she has no time to join church clubs and Ladies' Aid Societies, and talk scandal," said the irrepressible Milly Brown. "But I guess you'll soon have a new member any way for your society—because Hannah Burke Starks has come home and is occupying the Powell place adjoining us. You remember her don't you Mrs. Phillips."

"Well, I should say, "replied Mrs. Phillips, "she married young Dr. Stark of Cleveland. So she's home. Is her husband with her?"

"Oh no, she is a widow" said Milly, "and I'm thinking a pretty wealthy one at that."

"You don't say," said Mrs. Tucker. "How do you know?"

"Well, by the style of her and the way she lives and the improvements she is making in the place. She has house servants, a gardener, and chauffeur and a man to tend the farm and she has had the house all done over. You won't know the place when it is finished. And she has an immense touring car, and the dearest coupe she runs herself. Then she rides and has a beautiful thoroughbred horse and has just the finest of clothes."

"Well," said Mrs. Phillips, "that don't sound like she'll be much of a church worker—but we'll wait and see. You never can tell."

"Alice says she's lovely," replied Milly. "She's been very good to Alice."

"We must call," said Mrs. Tucker, "it is so lonely out there."

"Yes, it's lonely with only Milly and her Alice for neighbors" retorted Mrs. Phillips. "But I'll have to study over it first. You see I knew Hannah before she was married, and she was always a mighty independent little piece and held her head very high."

"Oh, that's nothing," said Mrs. Tucker, "birds fly high too, but they always come down for water. So perhaps your Hannah was lonesome and home-sick for the sight of home and old faces, the reason she returned to St. Michaels."

"Well—we'll soon see," said Mrs. Phillips. And see they did in a way that didn't suit St. Michaels folks at all.

The following Thursday the Ladies' Aid met at Mrs. St. Anthony's. They always met at Mrs. St. Anthony's whenever they could—and that was nine times out of ten—because her home was just a few steps below the parsonage and they could see Rev. Steele whenever he came out or in or had visitors, and then being close—he sometimes dropped in and took tea with the ladies, only when he came they served cocoa and tea cakes because it was more fashionable.

But this Thursday they were doomed to disappointment because Rev. Steele came out his gate—and every girl and old maid's heart beat a little faster, and each one either took her little chamois and touched up her nose a little for fear it might be shiny or patted her hair a little smoother or tucked a hair pin a little tighter—but with a gasp, of astonishment—instead of turning in at Mrs. St. Anthony's and sauntering slowly up the walk as usual—he walked briskly by without so much as a glance at the house.

The Ladies' Aiders sat as though paralyzed—and little Marie

Phillips, who thought he was on the eve of proposing to her, said, "Well the nerve of him. I wonder where he can be going?"

"Well if you say so," said Lillian Tucker, "I'll run and ask him."

"Now girls," said Miss Sara Simpson "don't get excited, you know a pastor of a church like ours has so many important duties to attend to that he can't always attend our meetings."

"Don't make excuses Sara," retorted Mrs. Phillips, "there isn't anything more important than our meetings."

"Stung," laughed Lillian Tucker—"perhaps he has gone to see the great and beautiful widow Stark"—and as though she had been a prophetess—the widow and the pastor came into view quietly talking and seemingly interested only in each other.

Everybody looked and if only the pastor could have known each ones' thought of him—who watched him so closely. The young girls were mostly amused but the spinsters and married women were not so charitably inclined.

Mrs. Stark was dressed in a fashionable tailor made suit with hat, gloves, and shoes to match and carried an armful of beautiful hot-house tea roses.

At his gate they stopped and she put out her hand and took his and put all the roses in them—and then she stooped and buried her face in them as though loath to part with them and when she raised her face he said something to her and buried his face in them as she had done.

"Look," said Miss Sara Simpson with a look of disgust on her face—"he is kissing and caressing them because she did so—right out in the street isn't it disgusting, and he seems to like her too and here last Sunday he took us to task about expensive clothes, and street walking and flirting and love-making in public and—"

"Do hush Sara," said Mrs. St. Anthony. "Look at the bunch of roses, it hasn't cost a cent less than $5. I imagine I can smell them here. I wonder if he really likes roses?"

Mrs. Tucker seemed genuinely amused at some unspoken thought and her quick light laugh—fell jarringly upon the members.

"Oh dear!" said one, "do keep quiet."

"I don't see anything to laugh about," said another.

"Well he likes roses well enough to keep those," said someone else.

"It seems so," said another.

The gate clicked shut and Mrs. Stark walked along up the street, unconscious of the storm she had stirred up.

"If she is so intimate with him, it's a wonder she wouldn't come to church and help with the church work or join the society and help to do something, and she wouldn't have time to flirt with the minister," said Mrs. St. Anthony.

"Has anyone"—asked Mrs. Phillips—"asked Hannah Stark to join our society or one of our church clubs?"

No one had—

"I'll do it now," said Mrs. Phillips.

"Hurry or she'll be out of sight," they urged. They followed Mrs. Phillips to the door.

Mrs. Stark had gone by—but she came back with a smile on her face, and not a little amused at being accosted thus. Mrs. Phillips stood on the top step and resolved to do what she thought was her duty.

"I am Mrs. Phillips—Mrs. Stark, and remember you as Hannah Burke—we saw you talking to Rev. Steele"—she said by way of introduction—"We thought you might like to join our society or our young people's Helping Hand Club."

Mrs. Phillips was unaware how she spoke—her voice cut the air like a whip saw—and said plainly—we do not want you, but you should think it your duty, — and an honor, that I, Mrs. Lawyer Phillips, should ask you to join.

Mrs. Stark's eyes snapped—and her head went up a little higher—"Thank you"—she said—"I feel honored. Does your pastor belong to these clubs and is he a member of the Church Aid Society?"

"No," exclaimed indignant Mrs. Phillips.

"Then I'm sorry to decline the honor, but I can't possibly belong to anything of which he is not a member, and not under his direct supervision."

She was gone, and Mrs. Phillips had to be helped in the house to the couch, and Mrs. St. Anthony was so angry she was blue in the face. I thought she would explode, and poor Miss Sara Simpson fainted; in fact everybody was out of commission but Mrs. Tucker, who got on everybody's nerves by laughing and saying—

"I like that woman. She's got spunk and brains enough to give you a dose of nicely sugar-coated pills that helps immensely."

Before night all St. Michaels had heard the story of the roses and the invitation to join the club and it did not lose anything in the telling.

Unconsciously, all St. Michaels formed a detective bureau to watch the pastor.

They played detective and they watched poor Rev. Steele's every move and at last they had come to the conclusion that he was hopelessly in love with the widow.

Poor Mrs. Stark did she know how St. Michaels regarded her, or what they thought of her? If she did—no one in St. Michaels was any the wiser.

Then one Sunday morning just a few weeks before Xmas, Mrs. Stark appeared at church, and the Ladies' Aid members that were present, I'm afraid paid more attention to Mrs. Stark than they did to the sermon, in fact I'm afraid they could not have given the sermon's text if asked—but I'm sure they could have told you all about Mrs. Stark's costume.

At the Thursday afternoon meeting following, Mrs. Stark was the topic as usual.

"What's wrong with her now," said Mrs. Tucker. "At first she was just a butterfly and a flirt, then she was haughty and proud, then she did not attend church, she was a heathen, now she attends church, you are still faultfinding and she is a hypocrite—what is wrong with her now?" she challenged.

"Well she is not a member," said Mrs. Phillips, "and she just came to have the pastor walk her home."

"Well whose business is it if she does. Don't you think Rev. Steele is old enough to look after himself?" said Mrs. Tucker.

"Well, what do you expect of us? You'd be suspicious yourself—after those roses—if you were not so in love with both her and the pastor, that it takes all your time to champion her cause and snub your neighbors, all on account of a city woman, who is supposed to have plenty of money and fine clothes. I think she's bewitched you," remarked Mrs. Phillips, "as you have gone clean daft about her."

"Well I'm satisfied," retorted Mrs. Tucker. "My opinion of the matter that we will lose all the ground we've gained—and waste our profits—if we don't stop this unseasonable, unreasonable squabbling—come to our senses and adjust the differences which have suddenly sprung up between the pastor and this society all on account of his attention to a woman, and we are not sure that he is paying special attention to her. Because a man calls on a woman or walks home with her is no sign he wants to marry her."

"Quite a sermon Mrs. Tucker, have you taken the Rev. Steele's place? Who elected you his champion," sarcastically asked Mrs. St. Anthony. "Perhaps the members here are not to your liking and you wish to resign."

"I am not trying to take anyone's place," retorted Mrs. Tucker— "but three weeks from now is Xmas, and this is hold together time— not hold-up or split-up time. A similar opportunity to have a big Xmas fete in the church and to get and keep all the younger folks working may never occur again and I move we take time by the forelock and get busy."

"The pastor gave those roses to old Mother Carey," explained Mrs. Tucker triumphantly, "and I bet Mrs. Stark knew all about it—perhaps she sent them by him."

"Humph!" said Miss Sara Simpson, "Jonathan Steele is a sly one—probably his pricking conscience told him the Ladies' Aid was watching."

Part II

"The marriageable women of our church are nice and would be a plus for any man. They are as pretty and dutiful as he'll find elsewhere, but he won't marry one of them. He can't see the pot over the sill of the window for the rain," said Mrs. Phillips. "If there was another church here we would leave, my husband says."

"And I would follow you," said Mrs. St. Anthony and Mrs. Ford in chorus—and then the trouble started.

Rev. Steele called a meeting of the Mite Society—and Ladies'

Aid Society—and organized a Young People's Get-together for Wednesday evening at 7 o'clock.

Although the three organizations consisted of seventy-five or more members among them, only five young folks and three old ones turned out—Millie Brown, Mrs. Tucker and Mrs. Ford.

Rev. Steele made no comment on the presence or the absence of the members.

"Well," said he, "this will be my first meeting with you, and as you have all been faithful the past seven months, I thought with your help—we will have a Xmas this year that will leave a sweet memory to every person at St. Michaels as long as life itself."

"Are you willing to help?"

"We certainly are," exclaimed Mrs. Tucker and the rest acquiesced.

Several committees were appointed and those who were absent, were notified of their appointments and the jobs they were expected to do.

Some agreed half-heartedly and some refused point blank to not only serve on the committees, but to attend church—and a split in the church of St. Michaels loomed large on the horizon.

Sunday morning two weeks before Xmas, Rev. Steele preached his second formal sermon in St. Michaels Church on "Gossip" and truly St. Michaels was in an up-heaval.

No one knew if he was aware of the feelings of his congregation or not. He had chosen "Gossip" for his subject, but in the middle of his sermon he told his congregation that no matter what happened—even if he was to render his resignation within the next twelve hours—he would have the satisfaction of knowing that he had been a p-a-s-t-o-r and not a figure head.

He got everyone to thinking and Mrs. St. Anthony wondered if "he could rightly know what had been said about him by the Ladies' Aid."

"It makes no difference if he does," said Mrs. Phillips. "It would do him not to know what I think of him."

"Humph," said Mrs. Tucker, "much he cares for your opinion or any one of the rest of us, I'm thinking. He believed Rev. Butler to be led by the nose wheresoever a set of crazy men and women choose to lead him."

When Frank Coombs resigned as superintendent of the Sunday School, they thought he'd be coaxed to remain, but when no one coaxed, only a few old heads—and Harry Young was asked to fill his place—it was like stirring up a hornet's nest. "Mrs. Coombs and her sister, Mrs. Cook, do come to church—but I declare they would be better at home," said Mrs. Ford.

"Mrs. Cook told me," said Mrs. Phillips, "she looked at the pipes of the organ so long and so hard that she could tell every move on them and where, with her eyes shut, and it was no wonder they had not fallen down on her before this."

"Old Mrs. Lake sits with the book up-side down—and pretends to read, when we all know she can't tell A from B if they were a yard high. Even the members of the Trustees' and Stewards' Boards are at logger heads, because he appointed some young men, who have lately joined the church, on the boards and asked for the resignation of some of the old men on the board. They had been on the board so long they were moss-covered."

"Well I can't see," said Mrs. St. Anthony, "why he wanted to change things around."

"I can tell you," said Mrs. Tucker, "he thinks if you want to keep young people in the church after they join—you should put them to work and make them feel they are wanted. You see it's useless to try to hold young folks anywhere now-a-days unless they have something to do. There is too much of this wanting to be boss all the time and a few old fogies wanting the church to stay in a rut and keeping things like they were fifty years ago. Times are changing and you've simply got to change with them or get out of the running. A piece of antique china is admired for its age—but it is put upon the shelf for safe keeping and admired for what it was and is not for its present use. So it is with us, we must either help the younger folks along or stand to be put on the shelf. I say live and let live."

"The whole thing in a nut-shell is he hasn't paid the attention to our marriageable daughters we thought he should," said Mrs. Tucker. "He goes among us—loves us—and thinks for our interest—which should make him loved by all—but it seems there must always be a few discontented ones among the flock."

"What's the use of jangling," said Mrs. Todd. "Let us get busy. What will you give towards the Christmas fete, Mrs. Hunter?"

"I—oh, don't know" said Mrs. Hunter—"I guess 2 quarts of cream and a chocolate cake."

"What will you give, Mrs. Phillips?"

"Not one single thing," she replied, "count me out of it. Mr. Phillips says we'll not take part in the affair."

"What will you give Mrs. Tucker."

"A cake, a chicken, 2 lbs. of coffee and help to do whatever I can."

"And you Mrs. Ford?"

"Oh—Mr. Ford says we'll not take any part in it."

"Look here ladies, before I go any further," said Mrs. Todd, "let me ask you that won't help, please do not hinder."

"Goodness gracious—Margery Todd put that list up—and don't use the Ladies' Aid's time for such foolishness," said Mrs. Phillips.

"Alright," said Mrs. Todd, "but I'll call on every one of you tomorrow."

"I can't get over that sermon," said Mrs. St. Anthony—hopping back to the old subject.

"Neither can I," said Mrs. Phillips.

"There goes the Reverend and the widow now!" said Marie Phillips.

"Well that caps the climax," said old Mrs. Ford bitterly, as the Reverend and the widow passed out of sight.

But she was mistaken. Something happened a few days later that threw the community into a tizzy. The whole community began to talk to each other through back doors, across to their neighbors, or talked across fences—back and front by the hour. They even called special meetings to discuss it, in fact everybody you met was talking about it and everybody held a squared white envelope which contained a beautifully printed square white card which was drawn out and compared with other cards just like it, and soon St. Michaels awoke to the fact that every member and non-member of St. Michaels, men, women and young people—was invited to an elaborate Christmas party.

In the words of Mrs. Tucker—"Mrs. Stark was giving a big Christmas blow out."

After the first surprise was over, everybody was wondering why he or she had been invited and one and all came to the conclusion, to get in with St. Michaels' folks—except the Ladies' Aid—who said Mrs. Stark was taking this way to show she was sorry for the way she had acted.

Though, Mrs. Tucker says—"What she had to be sorry for was beyond her."

Then came the getting ready for the party. The boy that blew the mouth organ thought his checkered pants and blue coat with his new tan shoes was just the thing. The sexton's wife bought a pretty white dimity dress—much too tight and which seemed to make her look twice as broad. But the leaders of the church—the—Ladies' Aid—such a flurry—such a bustling.

Of course Mrs. St. Anthony, Mrs. Phillips—the lawyer's wife, and the doctor's wife, Mrs. Jameson—and Miss Simpson and Mrs. White, and their daughters could and did go to the city to get their outfit, and as Marie Phillips told Mrs. Tucker the dresses will be real creations of art.

But the rest of St. Michaels had to be content to buy in St. Michaels, and to trust to Millie Brown, Violet Cunningham, and old Mrs. Thomas to make them.

Said Mrs. Tucker—"I'm mighty glad I'm invited—and I'm satisfied with any old plum-colored silk, because it's no use to go to that party trying to out dress Mrs. Stark, because she knows how to dress, and as Mr. Tucker says, she could put on my old plum-colored silk and look like an angel in it, with that mop of hair as black as a raven's wing and eyes as black as coal and a complexion like a rose leaf—she looks like a big doll anyway. I'll dress to suit Mrs. Tucker who is short and inclined to stoutness and past forty-five and not like Hannah," with which common sense remarks.

Mrs. Tucker took her ancient plum-colored silk and sewed

some real lace in the sleeves and fixed a dainty white fichu around the neck which would tend to make her look decidedly sweet and motherly and altogether lovely.

The wonderful night rolled around all too quickly, they went in conveyances of all kinds—wagons, ancient carriages, buggies, daytons, and autos, all carried their quota of guests.

But Mrs. Tucker and Mrs. Todd said the street cars were good enough for them so accompanied by Mr. Tucker and Mr. Todd, they wended their way there.

Everybody went—not one invitation was refused or ignored—they were there to eat, to listen, to enjoy, and above all to see how Rev. Steele and Mrs. Stark would act before the people of St. Michaels.

When they arrived, they were more than surprised at the display that met their gaze, and they were awed into silence—and as they gazed, they, one and all, thought how beautiful.

Even Mrs. St. Anthony and Mrs. Phillips and Miss Simpson who were used to such things, had never seen anything quite as elaborate as this. Whatever else they may think, there was only one thing that could be said of her in regards to this Christmas party—it was gotten together on an elaborate scale and it was well done.

When they entered, they were turned over to the maid who took them upstairs and ushered them into a room, where wraps were removed and checked and they had a chance to pin back a stray strand of hair or adjust a ribbon if they so wished, then when returning down stairs were announced by the butler—who was none other than young Bill Winston, hired and dressed up for the occasion, and who walked so straight and held his head so high that they wondered if he could see the folks he announced.—They entered timidly and in nervous little groups, following each other sheep-fashion, to the place where the hostess stood to receive them—not knowing, the most of them, whether to shake hands or simply bow, nor what to do with themselves afterwards.

But once the hostess greeted them they forgot their self-consciousness and their nervousness in looking at the vision of loveliness that had greeted them. She wore a lovely dress—"a most wonderful gown," Mrs. Tucker said, "of some sort of white stuff—that looked soft, billowy clouds of fleece—dotted here and there with stones that shone like hundreds of stars and sparkled like thousands of diamonds under the blazing electric light;" and as Old Mrs. Ford said, "she made everybody feel so homey and comfortable."

"Well I declare," said Mrs. Phillips, "a bridal costume as I live"—as she gazed at the little spray of orange blossoms that nestled so lovingly in Mrs. Stark's abundant dark hair.

"Do you know," said Sara Simpson. "I believe she has invited us all to her wedding."

Someone whispered, "Isn't she glorious?" And it floated from one to the other around the room, there was a gentle hum as of bees in the distance, everybody seemed happy.

"I wonder where the Reverend is?" said old Mrs. St. Anthony.

Time passed and the older folks commenced to get restless—the younger ones were in dream-land and as the orchestra music was wafted so softly and temptingly on the air the younger folks looked longingly at the waxed floor glistening in the distance and wished the pastor would not show up so they could dance.

"Oh!" said Marie Phillips, "just for one turn on that floor"— and the rest echoed her wish.

People commenced to move nervously about, and to stand and

talk in excited little groups. There was a hint of something in the air that no one could tell what it was—where was Rev. Steele? Why didn't the wedding take place? Who was going to marry them?

Even Mrs. Stark was getting restless, her cheeks were flushed, and her eyes fairly glistened and kept roaming toward the side entrance. Her hands played nervously with her fan—the young folks were almost tempted to ask could they dance.

The time seemed to pass so slowly and a wave of restlessness hard to control was fast gaining possession of the guests.

Everybody took to cautiously watching Mrs. Stark, who was walking aimlessly here and there around the rooms and talking nervously to first one guest and then another, but it was noticed that her glance wondered continually toward the side entrance, the music itself seemed to accelerate the restlessness of the crowd.

Suddenly the music changed—as the strains of Lohengrin's Wedding March pealed joyously forth—the side door was thrown wide and the footman announced in a stentorian voice—"Mr. and Mrs. Jonathan Steele."

Everybody turned to look, and there standing framed in the doorway, smilingly stood the Rev. Jonathan Steele, and standing by his side—clinging to his arm stood his bride—timid little Alice Brown, in a simple white dress, looking for all the world like a happy Brown Thrush.

Of course everybody in the room could have told you, that they knew it was Alice Brown the pastor had been coming out into the lonely end of town to see.

And all the girls and spinsters who had held high hopes of becoming the pastor's wife, will tell you that Rev. Steele is a passably good-looking man, but he is a long way from being a handsome one.

"Sour grapes," says Mrs. Tucker. But the Ladies' Aid and the Helping Hand ladies just looked at Alice's mother Milly Brown, and wondered to themselves how she ever kept it to herself.

But it did not matter, only to a few like Miss Sara Simpson— whose chances of finding a husband were getting fewer each year and to Mrs. Phillips—who was anxious to see Marie safely settled, and to Mrs. St. Anthony, who could not now meddle so easily in the pastor's household affairs. To the majority, he had married a St. Michaels girl and that was the main thing, so the church was decorated, good things donated, and the Christmas fete was a royal reception to the pastor and his bride. And to this day St. Michaels' folks love to tell of the Christmas party and how it prevented a split in the church.

THREE MEN AND
A WOMAN
Augustus M. Hodges

Augustus Hodges used social criticism to explore key themes in the African American experience during the 1890s and engaged controversial subjects of the time, such as interracial relations, lynching, miscegenation, racial stereotyping, white liberalism, the "New South," and racism. "Three Men and a Woman" has a didactic tone, as Hodges assumes the role of commentator addressing these topics.

The story hinges around three Christmas Eves, the first in 1890, when the plot is hatched for Ella Watson, a young white woman, to get rid of her husband, Clarence Watson, and to trick her elderly white paramour, Captain Harry Seabergh, into giving her two thousand dollars so that she can be with Jerry Stratton, her black lover. Ella is the granddaughter of Nathan Bedford Forrester, a slave owner, importer of slaves from Africa, celebrated Confederate army general, and the founder of the Klu Klux Klan, which arose in Tennessee following the end of the Civil War.

The first seven chapters of "Three Men and a Woman" describe how Ella and Stratton accomplish their goal. However, Ella, who later marries Stratton, is not content to just stay in New

York with him. She longs to visit her relatives in South Carolina. She convinces Stratton, a naive native-born New Yorker, to go to South Carolina with her, where they discover that the "New South," so highly touted in the press, is infested with a virulent racism that is intolerant of interracial relationships.

The essential question raised by Hodges is what is the significance of Christmas to white Southerners? Do they have a "profound reverence and respect for the birthday of Christ," as Stratton believes, or will they "commit murder on a holy day like Christmas or Good Friday?"

In "Three Men and a Woman," Hodges effectively addresses the most salient issues of the time. He explodes the myth of black men raping white women and demonstrates that race supersedes any notion of American democratic ideals when the issue is the virtue of white womanhood, that the same forces in control during the antebellum period are in power after the Civil War, and that both miscegenation and violence against Southern blacks are widespread. Hodges's interest in interracial love and the problems inherent in such relationships is in part related to his marriage in the 1890s to a Canadian white woman, who was disowned by her family for marrying a black man.

"Three Men and a Woman" is a fascinating story that falls outside the genre of short stories written and published by black writers of the time. Few black newspaper editors would have published a story such as this. Interestingly, the story's serialization in the *Indianapolis Freeman* (1902–1903) ends abruptly after the publication of chapter 10, in which the town leaders have decided to lynch Stratton and Uncle Tom. The newspaper did not explain why the story was being discontinued, and readers were left with a cliffhanger. It is probable that the story, especially chapter 10, caused quite a stir with Booker T. Washington and his supporters, who would have viewed the depiction of "leading" white citizens as the architects, perpetrators, and manipulators of much of the lynching and violence against Southern blacks as highly dangerous. It is likely that the readers demanded an ending to the story, causing the *Indianapolis Freedman* to reconsider its decision and complete publication.

Three Men and a Woman

Chapter I THE THREE MEN
AND THE WOMAN

The time was the year of our Lord 1890, "the night before Christmas;" the place was New York City; the section was No.——West Forty-ninth street, near Fifth avenue. The place was a "Raine's Law" hotel and ladies' cafe, a place where "respectable" women (white of course) slipped in to have a drink during the day (or night) while their husbands were at work or business; in short, it was a gilded place of vice, "only this and nothing more"—a first class place of its kind.

The hour was 8 at night, while all outside was life and business; inside was dull and deserted. Christmas Eve, almost everybody in Greater New York over 10 years old can be found upon the streets until midnight, either buying Christmas presents or looking at others buy them.

Inside of the "Admiral Cafe," as the back room of the hotel and bar room was called, marched up and down, a colored man, who the layman would call a plain waiter, but who considered himself (and was so registered) as night clerk and steward. He was of a dark brown complexion, little above the medium height, with unmistakable, but "fine" Negro features. His hair, which was of the three quarter blooded Negro grade, was cut short behind and long on top; it was well combed, brushed and oiled, and together with his faultless full dress suit made him look like a statesman, literary man or man of wealth, instead of—what he was.

As he walked the floor from one end to the other, he constantly looked at his gold watch. The echo of his steps resounded upon the marble-tiled "checker board" pattern of the floor. After walking up and down for an hour, he pulled out his watch and remarked to himself: "'Tis quarter to eight and she—"

Just then the street door opened and a pretty young white woman—a blonde—a picture for an artist to paint, entered the cafe— followed by a man below the average in size and mental looks. The colored waiter advanced towards the woman with an extended hand and smile upon his face. She winked her eyes, placed her fore finger across her lips, and remarked in a cold commanding tone: "Waiter, give me a 'Bill of Fare' until I see what my husband and I will have for supper." (Great stress was placed—with a wise look—upon the words, "My husband!") The colored attendant put on a sober, business like look and handed the woman a bill of fare. She looked over it a moment, passed it to her husband and without waiting for him to make his selection, said: "Waiter, give us two portions of 'Lobster-a-la-Newbergh' and a bottle of claret." The waiter (as we will hereafter, in this chapter, call the colored man) went to the rear of the cafe, where he yelled the order for the lobster down stairs to the cook. He then went to the bar room where he got the bottle of claret, which he served in the latest style. In a few minutes a colored kitchen attendant brought the lobster and "trimmings" up from the kitchen and turned them over to the waiter, who served the same in great style. He had just done so when the door opened and a stately old man entered. A screen behind the door prevented his seeing in the room.

"Hello Jerry! has that friend of mine—"

The colored waiter raised a warning hand, winked his eye and placed his finger over his lips. The old man took the hint and finished his sentence with: "That friend of mine, Mr. Hopkins, been here to-night?"

"No sir," was the reply.

The old man walked down the cafe and seated himself at a middle row table opposite the woman and her husband. He exchanged looks with the woman, but no one could tell from their looks that they had ever seen each other before. The old man ordered "a small bottle," and made it last until the woman and her husband were gone. A description of the old man is needful: He was a tall, soldierly looking man over six feet, with hair and mustache as white as snow; and ideal picture of the "Silver King" in that well known play bearing that name, or the mythical "Kentucky Colonel," of whom the funny men of the newspapers write so many jokes about. He was dressed in spotless black, with a long Prince Albert coat and high hat, with a deep widower's band.

The waiter looked at his male guest from head to foot, then went to the mirror and looked at himself. It could be plainly seen that he concluded, that he was the best and most attractive looking of the three men; and he was.

The woman and her husband having finished their supper, she remarked to him: "Wait, my dear, until I find out where the ladies' dressing room is and wash my hands and fix my hair." Turning to the waiter, she asked: "Waiter, where is the ladies' dressing room?"

She was standing with her back toward both men, and she winked her eye and passed a note to the waiter as he was directing her to the dressing room she well knew.

A few minutes after she and her husband left the room, and the colored waiter hastened to read the note. It was printed, or written in capital letters with a pencil, and was in cipher.

It read:

TELL 'NO. 2' TO MEET 'NO. 4' AT PARKER'S
RESTAURANT AT 10 O'CLOCK, AS 'NO. 3'
GOES TO BRIDGEPORT IN A HOUR. TELL
'NO. 1' TO MEET 'NO. 4' AT 1 O'CLOCK
AT THIRTY-THIRD STREET AND SIXTH
AVENUE. HAVE A CAB. 'NO. 4.'

Immediately after reading the note, the waiter went over to the old man and said: "Ella says meet her at Parker's at 10 o'clock, Capt."

"Is that her husband?" asked the old man.

"That—is—her—husband," slowly replied the waiter, as he walked away to wait upon other patrons, as the place was beginning to fill up with night patrons. At half past twelve the waiter was "off duty," and after giving instructions to the man who took his place, he quickly put on his street clothes and hurried out to the corner of Thirty-third street and Sixth avenue, where he hired a cab; soon after the woman came up to the corner. She and the waiter entered the cab and were driven, by the waiter's direction, to a house in West Sixteenth street, kept by a colored woman.

The three men and the woman, just spoken of, are the foundation of our story.

Chapter II THE "WOMAN"

Mrs. Ella Watson, whose maiden name was Forrester, was the granddaughter of one of the worst "nigger" hating slaveholders and rebels that South Carolina ever produced before the Civil war. She was born in C___ , South Carolina, twenty-three years before our opening chapter. Her father was a drummer boy in the Confederate army, and her grandfather a general in the same "lost cause." She had from infancy been taught to hate the Negro and treat him as an inferior, and did so until she reached the age of reason and was a graduate from one of the leading high schools for "F. F. V." young ladies in the mother state of Virginia. The kindness of a male Negro servant, during her last year at the Virginia high school, convinced Ella Forrester that "niggers" were not as black as her people had painted them; that they were human beings like the whites; that they did not make or select their race or color; that their color and birth place (like her own) were the accidents of nature or fate. She at once resolved to treat Negro people as well as she did white people in the same walks of life.

Like all progressive, educated American young women, she did her own thinking, and often wished that the accident of birth had placed her north of the "Mason and Dixon's line," as the granddaughter of a private Union Civil War soldier, instead of the granddaughter of a Confederate general. She visited an uncle residing in Boston and noticed the vast progressive difference between the old North and the "New South," and resolved to make the progressive North her home. Her folks would not agree to this, so she, with a faithful Negro maid, ran away from the God forsaken state of South Carolina to that portion of "God's country" known as New York City, three years before our opening chapter. Her education secured for her a position as book keeper in one of the leading dry goods stores in Greater New York. After she had been with the firm for one year; after she had become a full fledged New York girl; after she had learned its faults and its fashions, its sins and its pleasures; after she had concluded that she would not exist outside of Greater New York, the firm in which she was employed, failed, and she found herself without a penny. She "knew the ropes" by this time, and concluded to get married, as a married woman's certificate (in New York City) covers a multitude of sins, so she took unto herself a husband.

Chapter III   THE "HUSBAND"

Clarence Watson was a native of New York City, a printer by trade— a member of the "big six," and an employee upon one of the leading New York City morning newspapers at the time of our opening. He was one of Greater New York's bread winners, who put all confidence in his wife's honesty in keeping her marriage vows. A year after—twelve months of happy married life—there was a "strike" upon the paper upon which he worked, and the printers' places were filled with non union men, and Watson found himself "on the town" with house rent due. His wife came to his aid, and for several days (and nights) went to see her relatives (so she said) and each time "borrowed" two or five dollars. They lived on the "borrowed" (nightly) money for several months, when it dawned upon Watson that his wife was not getting the money from her relatives. He had by this time got used to a life of easy living; in which he had his house rent paid, plenty to eat, plenty to drink and money in his pocket to spend.

We all recall the story about the Quaker who told his son: "My son, thee must have money to get along in this world; get it honestly if thou can, but—get it." Clarence Watson soon became a student of this school of philosophy. When he asked his wife for two or five dollars and she handed it to him, he did not ask her where or in what way she got it. In all large cities in the North and West the majority of the men are bread winners—sons of toil—still there is also a large minority who "toil not, neither do they spin," yet they have all the good (and bad) things of life provided by their wives' earnings, and they do not or dare not question the manner in which the money was earned. Watson soon drifted into this class, and when the strike was over and the union printers returned to their cases, he failed to answer the roll call. He informed his fellow workmen that he was living on "Easy Street," and was out of the business. He became a full fledged "sport," "played the races" and "poker" upon the money his wife gave him. When a woman gets a man to this degree, she (womanlike) rules him with an iron hand. When Mrs. Watson wanted him to go out for the night, she ordered him out, and—he went. When she wanted him to stay in the house, she ordered him to stay, and he did so.

Chapter IV   THE "OLD MAN"

Capt. Harry Seabergh was, at our opening, a man of sixty-four, a German by birth, who came to this country with his parents when he was four years old. His father was a civil engineer and a man of money, who gave his son a good high school education and then sent him to Yale, where he graduated with honors. His father died the day the son was twenty-one, and the mother six months later. Young Seabergh possessed his father's wealth which he invested in Brooklyn real estate, which paid him about three hundred per cent. He went to the Civil War a captain in Company C, 99th N. Y. Volunteer, and was a brave soldier. He married and was the father of six daughters, five of whom were married at the date of the opening of this story, and all of them older than "the woman in the case." His wife, who had been a helpless invalid for three years, died seven months before the beginning of this romance. He knew she was dying and went after a doctor, met Ella Watson, flirted with her and took her to the "Admiral Cafe" and bought her a "wine supper." When he returned his wife was dead. It has often been said by women in a position to know, that "an old fool is the worst fool of all," and Captain Seabergh was a living proof that this statement was true to the letter. In the language of the street, Ella Watson "worked him for all he was worth." He gave her hundred dollar bills, bought her diamonds and pearls and fine dresses, and kept the wolf from Mr. and Mrs. Watson's door for many moons.

Chapter V   THE "WAITER"

Jerry Stratton was born in New York City, where his father and mother also first saw the light of day. His mother's maternal parents were Long Island Shinnecock Indians, his father's parents being full blooded Virginians of direct African parentage. He was thirty years old at the time he was introduced to the reader in our opening chapter. He was a graduate of the Brooklyn High School, and had been a law student. He never finished his law course, as the alluring money making position at the "Admiral Hotel" (where he first went for the summer to earn his winter's school money) made him a slave of the "almighty dollar." He was an up-to-date New York City man, no better and no worse than the average man, black or white.

He is the hero, not the angel, of this story, as it has no angels in it. This is not a Sunday school story, although it is a Christmas one. At the time of our writing there were few angels in New York City; human nature and the devil had "cornered the market" in angels.

This romance is written something on the Emile Zola style, to wit: It deals in life as found to-day in the United States, and shows some of the true relationships of the two races. It is an attempt to prove that the white people of the country (the South especially) are not as pure as they paint themselves, nor the black people as immoral and as bad as the "white folks" paint them.

Chapter VI   KEEPING ENGAGEMENTS

After the woman and her husband left the Admiral Cafe, she hurried him towards the Grand Central depot. He remarked on the way: "Ella, I don't think I'll go to Bridgeport for that job, but try and get one here; I don't want to be so far away from you." The woman looked at him with a firm, commanding look, and replied. "Well, I think you will go there on the next train, or go to the devil. I am not going to house and feed you any longer. You have got to hustle or starve, as my dream of love is over. Here goes your train," and she almost pushed him on the car. She waited until the train left the depot and then hurried down to Parker's Cafe to meet Capt. Seabergh.

He was on time waiting. They entered Parker's, where the old man ordered a private dining room and a "wine supper" at a cost of $25. After the supper and the wine had been served the old man (we started to call him "old fool," but our literary position forbids us from so doing) upon his knees, pleaded to her to leave her husband and go with him. Leave him honorably if she would, (that is, get a divorce) or dishonorably if she must. His seemingly logic was thus: "Now Ella, you are too pretty, too young and too intelligent to spend your time with that beggar you call your husband. He is a man far below your standard, and it is a problem to me how you ever married him. Yes, it is the greatest problem of my life. Now, little girl, listen to me; 'shake' him—get a divorce from him or leave him in any way, honorable or dishonorable, and marry or live with me, and you will never want for this world's goods or pleasures, whether good or bad. What do you say, little girl?"

Ella laughed the laugh of a sharp "woman of the street" who knows her business, and remarked: "Oh you old sinner! Why is it you old 'lobsters' are always running after young girls almost young enough to be your granddaughters?"

"Love for 'the young and beautiful,' together with the incurable human nature we can't curb, my dear," was the old man's reply.

"I want some money to get a new dress and to spend. Give it to me now and to-night I will, upon my word, seriously think over your suggestion," said Ella.

"How much do you want, little girl," asked the old man, as he pulled out his well filled pocket book.

"Not much, only fifty dollars in small bills," was the reply.

He counted out fifty dollars and handed the same to her. She secreted the money in her stocking, then looked at the clock and remarked: "Well, I must go; I promised my husband to be home at twelve o'clock, and here it is half past the hour; will see you tomorrow night—bye, bye," and she arose.

"But, little girl, you know—"

"No 'buts,' I must go; remember I must spend some time with my husband," she remarked as she kissed the old man and hurried out to meet the colored waiter.

She boarded a Sixth Avenue street car and rode to Thirty-third street, where she found the colored waiter waiting with an engaged cab. She entered the cab before the driver saw her race and color, and having previously received his instructions, the driver drove to the house in West Sixteenth Street.

The front parlor was lighted when they went up the steps. The waiter rang the bell three times, when the lights at once went out, after which he took out of his pocket a key chain with a bunch of keys and picked out one, opened the front door and entered the dark parlor.

"Is that you Mr. Stratton," asked a voice from the hall.

"Yes mam, Mom," was the reply.

"Well go up to your rooms, they are ready."

With this information they walked up to the parlor and alcove above the ground floor, the best and most expensive rooms in the house. After taking off their coats and hats, Jerry (the waiter) remarked: "There is no place like home."

He rang the bell, and when a servant knocked and the door was opened, he remarked: "Tell Mom to send up a half dozen bottles of Peel's beer, two good cigars, (two for [a] quarter), a broiled chicken, a box of sardines, a bottle of 'Old Crow' whiskey and a package of cigarettes, and have them charged to me."

"Oh, Jerry!" said the woman, "don't have them charged to us, that looks so small for us." Turning to the servant, she said: "Here Sarah, tell 'Mom' to take it all out of this ten dollar bill, and tell her to have a drink on me—I mean Mr. Stratton—and take out a half dollar 'tip' for yourself, Sarah."

Sarah did as she was directed, and soon returned with the several articles and the scant remaining change from the ten dollar bill, when she retired and left the couple "alone in their glory" of disgrace.

After the better half of the food and liquor had been consumed, the colored waiter (who we will hereafter call by his name—Jerry Stratton) lit a cigar, then threw himself on the sofa, while the woman took a seat on a pillow on the floor near his head. She was also smoking—a Turkish cigarette—the kind that nine out of ten young white women of Greater New York smoke.

She smiled as she looked into her companion's face as she re-marked: "Say, Jerry, that old 'lobster' wants me to run away with him. Ha! ha! the old fool. He wants me to go out West with him—to California. He says he will give me all the money I want, and—"

"Why, that's dead easy; get a couple of thousands in cold cash from him, go with him as far as Chicago and then shake him, and come back to New York to me."

"I never thought of that, Jerry, I will do it."

"Say, you are dead slow, Ella. If I were a pretty girl like you—well say, I wouldn't do a thing to those old hay seeds."

Before morning the plot was completed. Ella Watson was to get all the cash she could get from the old man, get him to purchase two tickets to Oakland, California, desert him at Chicago and return to New York to her colored lover, which plan was carried out to the letter.

Chapter VII THE PLOT'S CONSUMMATION

What story is not full of woman's falsehood?
the sex is all a sea of wide destruction;
We are vent'rous barks, that leave our home
For some sure dangers which their smiles conceal.

—LEE.

Ella Watson went as far as Chicago with the old man; during the distance from New York to Chicago she blackmailed him into giving her two thousand dollars in small greenbacks. When she got to Chicago she "jumped" the train and returned to New York to her colored lover, Jerry Stratton. The old man was miles west of Chicago before he missed her, as she left him to go to the ladies dressing room to comb her hair (so she said.) He did not then realize that he had been "done." The colored Pullman car porter told him that he saw a lady running after the train pulled out of Chicago, and the old man concluded she had left the car and did not return before it started on its California journey. He expected her to follow on the next through train, but she did not. After he had been in Oakland, California two weeks, the truth dawned upon him.

When Ella Watson returned to New York she gave the money to her colored lover, who was diplomatic enough to immediately give it back to her, with the remark: "No, Ella, you keep it; you are the 'banker' of this firm, I am only the 'broker.' You hold the money. I'll do the rest, ha! ha!"

For five years Ella Watson and Jerry Stratton lived together in what they called "bliss." Woman is inconstant; man is changeable. The man of the world who is living an immoral life soon tires of his female toy and gets another one; the woman of the world—woman like—is never true to the man she is supposed to love. She has other toys with which she plays, but—she is careful not to let "a good thing" slip through her fingers. Ella Watson was "only a woman," with all the passions of womanhood of her class, and she rightly guessed that Stratton would soon tire of her, and unless she had some legal hold on him, he would leave her, she therefore resolved to marry him. New York State—God's country—a man or woman can marry the person they want, regardless of "race, color or previous condition." Ella Watson resolved to marry Jerry Stratton. In order to do so she was first obliged to get a divorce from her white husband. In order to do this she took a female companion in confidence—got her to lure Watson to New York City from Bridgeport, Connecticut, to the "Admiral Hotel," where the woman and Watson registered as "Mr. Amos B. Clark and wife." Soon after they had retired, Ella Watson and three witnesses (two of whom were detectives and the third one Jerry Stratton, her lover) broke in Watson's room and got the needful evidence for a divorce—which she got and married her colored lover. She was now Stratton's full-fledged wife with all of a New York state wife's rights. Jerry Stratton borrowed five hundred dollars from his wife the day after they were married and "played the races," winning nine hundred dollars more, all of which he gave her, with the exception of one hundred dollars. With this he played poker and won three hundred dollars more. He then concluded to give up his position at the "Admiral Hotel" and live the life of a sport, but he was afraid his wife (who had all the coin) would treat him as a dependent of charity. The problem of his mind was: "To leave work or not to leave." It was solved for him by the hotel burning down, or more properly speaking burning out, one morning when there was another fire in the same district and the engines were late in getting there. They moved in a "flat" house occupied by white people in One Hundred and Twenty-sixth street, West.

When they first moved in the flat which was a ground (or first floor one), and the neighbors saw Stratton's dark complexion, they raised an uproar at the idea of living under the same roof with a "nigger," but when Mrs. Stratton told them that she was Spanish and her husband a native of Cuba, who was seldom at home on account of his business, they accepted the situation and tried to be "chummy" neighbors. They did not have the opportunity to carry out their program, as the Stratton's were hardly ever home. They rented the flat, which they furnished in great style, simply to have a home, or more properly speaking, an asylum, where they could sleep one or two nights in the week when not elsewhere having "a good time."

Chapter VIII A VISIT TO THE "NEW SOUTH"

By personal agreement, Mr. and Mrs. Stratton agreed not to recognize each other when it was to their financial interests not to do so. In other words, they agreed that he would not recognize her if he met her on the street with a white person (male or female) that he did not know and she was not to recognize him if she met him on the street with a colored man (she drew the line at a colored woman) and he, fool-like or man-like, accepted the terms. About a year after this agreement, she went to the Grand Music Hall with a white man where, during the play, the song, "The Old Oaken Bucket" was sung, which aroused in her heart a desire to visit the scenes of her childhood.

When she returned home she told her husband—Jerry Stratton

of her desire and intentions to visit South Carolina and asked him to go with her.

He accepted. He was not well read upon the social conditions south of the Mason and Dixon Line, [since] he was of northern birth. He did not know that he was going into a lion's den of race prejudice, into a furnace of social fire, into the home of southern Confederacy, into the bed of rebellion, into the mouth of hell, into the devil's country instead of New York, God's country, that he was about to leave. Love or admiration for a woman makes a man blind as to the future, and—Jerry Stratton was blind. They secured Pullman car service to Knoxville, Tennessee, where they transferred to a Jim Crow line to Charleston, South Carolina. He was not aware of the change, as he made the acquaintance of a sporty colored man on the train, who led him into what he concluded was the smoking car, but which was in fact the Jim Crow car. As they were playing poker for money, and Stratton was (by fraud) winning, he did not notice that he was in a Jim Crow car and in ignorant bliss reached Charleston, S.C., twenty miles south of C____. During which time he won over three hundred dollars. When they reached Charleston, he and his white wife parted, by a suggestion of his own. He went with his new found friend to a den of vice and she to a fashionable hotel. He won about three hundred dollars at the card table, enough to pay for their visit South. She had a good time in Charleston, as a Northern lady. They then prepared to visit C ____ the home of her childhood. They hired a "hack" the Southern name for a broken down cab, or carriage, which was a hack indeed, drove to C____. His new found friend also went with him to C____. There Stratton and his wife parted, by agreement. Before he left New York City, he purchased several Remington and Winchester rifles, double barrel shotguns and a goodly supply of bird and bear shot and powder, all of which he soon found use for.

After trying to hunt on posted land for three days, during which time he learned the civil, social and political prejudice against his people, he gave it up as a bad job.

During this time his wife had been stopping at the farm of her great uncle's, five miles from the cross-road hamlet of C___ in the township bearing the same name. During her three days' stay at her great uncle's house, she learned the mistake she had made in leaving New York City, God's country, and revisiting C ___, the home of her childhood, the devil's land, or she saw her mistake in bringing with her, her Negro husband. Both husband and wife, without consultation or knowledge of each other, resolved to get back home at once—together if they could, separate if they must.

He engaged lodgings under the roof of a two-room log cabin, the home of the Negro who had acted as their guide, or protector, during their hunt on forbidden or posted ground. Jerry Stratton and his wife met, and resolved to return to New York City. "Jerry," she said, "I fear grave trouble for us, or at least you, as the prejudice against interracial social relations are as bitter here as they were one hundred years ago, however, as I led you into this trap I will get you out of it or—we will, more properly speaking, get out of it together. We will stop at your boarding house, at Uncle Tom's for the next few days and then quietly return to New York. Remember my love, [whatever happens,] I will live or die with you."

They passed the next four days in what the romantic author would call "Love's Young Dreams," or what the author of this story calls "blind love." It is a surprising fact to those who do not know the working of the rural districts, how news and gossip can fly so fast in a section of the country where there are no telegraphs or telephones. In three days it was known throughout C___ township, a radius of ten miles, that Nat Forrester's great niece was living with a "nigger" from the North below the village of C ___, in the log cabin of old "Uncle Tom Tatum," and of course the righteous (?) indignation of the country folks was aroused to action, and old man Forrester was told to talk to the girl and get her to leave the "nigger" after which the best citizens in the community would lynch the "nigger" and report it as a rape case for the good of the community.

Old Nat Forrester, who was three score and ten and an old Confederate soldier, sent word by a Negro boy to Ella Stratton, his great niece, that he wanted to have an immediate talk with her at his farm home. She, expecting treachery in some form, perhaps kidnapping, refused to go. Old Nat Forrester then rode down to Uncle Tom Tatum's cabin and called her out and remarked:

"Now see here, Ella, you's my brother's gran' darter an' I recon' I'se there only old member of our family. Now, I want ter to say ter you gal, that you have disgraced an honorable family of true blue [blooded] southern people by taken up with a nigger. I don't blame you gal, [cause you] is run away when you was young and I recon' you got mixed up with them d---- Yankees who thinks that niggers are as good as white folks, but they is not. Niggers is only like horses and mules—made to work for white folks. They are not human beings, they have no souls and were only made to be slaves before the war and servants now, they ------."

"Well Uncle Nat, if these people or brutes as you call them are not human, how is it that white men associate with women of this breed? How is it that two-thirds of these people have white blood in their veins? How is it that some 'niggers' as you call them are fairer than some whites? Have not 'niggers' who have white fathers souls? Are not 'niggers' who are as white as ourselves men and women?"

"Well---er---er---well, no; one drop of nigger blood in a person makes him a nigger."

"I cannot accept either your terms, logic or your appeal, so good day. You mind your own business and we will attend to ours. We will leave this God forsaken country in a few days, never to return."

With these words she shut the door into old Nat Forrester's face. With a heart full of grief this old gentleman of the "State Rights" state of South Carolina returned homeward. He stopped at the cross road hamlet, known as C____ village where he made his report, the result of which it was decided by five of the best citizens in the community that the girl would be sent to a private insane asylum, and the nigger be burned alive at the stake. So said Jack Nash, the lawyer, and everyone said "that's so." It was decided to burn Stratton at the stake after Christmas. Their deep reverence for the Christmas holidays only prevented them taking actions at once.

Chapter IX   FAREWELL PRAYER

"'Twas the night before Christmas," in the year of our Lord, 1897. The time a little after sunset, what they call in the Southland "candle light," that Uncle Tom Tatum rushed in his log cabin, where Jerry and Ella Stratton were stopping.

His face bore an excited and frightened look; his eyes protruded from his head; his nostrils expanded; his lips turned gray; his whole body shook with fear. It was several minutes before he could speak. He at last spoke: "Mister Strattum an' Mist Eller, fo' de Lawd sake; yes fo' hebben sake! please ter go' way; please ter leave my house;

please do' git there ole man inter trubble; please don't git me kilt; please—"

"What in thunder's the matter with you Uncle Tom? Are you drunk or crazy?"

"I'se nuther drunk nor crazy, but I wants ter tell yo' all deys comin' to lynch yo' after Christmuss ef dey finds yo' all here, an' dey may lynch me too, so please leave my house ter once. I'se sorry—mighty sorry, but I can't hope it."

"What are you talking about, Uncle Tom?" asked the woman.

"Why Missie yo' see its dis way: de white folks down here don't like ter see yo' messin' wid we black man. Taint right lees more dey don't think it is right. Dey don't like Mistar Strattum an' deys comin ter lynch him, less more, burn him up, less him and yo' gits out of there place ter once, or less more there day after Christmuss; so fer my sake please git out."

During this pleading the old man fell upon his knees, "Ef you' don't git out I must; but if I does I's lose all of my property."

Uncle Tom's "property," outside of the two room log cabin, which was built upon rented land, was an old bed, two broken chairs, an ax, a hoe, two spades, five plates, two cups, two knives and forks, one pot, one skillet, a sheep's gray home spun Sunday suit and a side of bacon: but they were his, and he did not want to loose them; and had also resolved not to loose his life protecting or harboring a stranger from the North upon whose head was the wrath and righteous (?) indignation of the "best white citizens of the community."

Jerry and Ella looked at each other while Uncle Tom walked up and down the floor in an excited manner. Stratton was the first to speak: "Now see here, Uncle Tom, we can't leave here for three or four days, at least before Christmas, so we will buy you out and pay cash. How much do you want for everything in the place you can not carry away; everything but your personal property? That is to say, to make it plain, what will you take for everything you cannot carry in a bag on your back, and what you can replace new with money?"

"Well," said the old man, after several minutes' reflection, "dey otter be worf $25." Seeing Stratton pull out of his pocket a large roll of bills, the old man added: "Less more dey otter be worf $30 what I leaves hind me. Dey otter—"

"Well, you sell me everything in the house, besides what you can carry away on your back, Uncle Tom, for $30?" asked Stratton.

"Yesser," replied Uncle Tom.

"Well, Uncle Tom, here is $100 in small bills, now escape for your life."

The old man stood for a few minutes in mute surprise, before he spoke: "Young man, I's sorry fer yo, but yo' orter knowed better than ter come down here with a white woman, less more if she is your wife. Yo's got eddykasun; yo' reads de papers; yo' knows how dey—there white folks—down here does our folks. I's an ole man 'bout seventy-five. I can't live much longer, but I does not want ter be lynched. I wants ter live out my time an' go to hebben when I dies. Is yo' got 'ligion or is yo' er sinner man, Mist Strattum?"

"Well, Uncle Tom, I am what you emotional Baptist and Methodist good folks would call a 'sinner man.' I have not got what you would call religion."

"Den I'se goin' ter pray fer yo' soul," replied Uncle Tom. He took off his hat, placed it upon the table, knelt down and motioned them, in a commanding way to kneel; they obeyed. All was silent for two or three minutes. It was silent prayer, (at least on the part of Uncle Tom). At last Uncle Tom began to pray in a low, solemn voice, clear and distinct. He pleaded with the "God of his fathers" not to forsake the American Negro, in this, the darkest hour in his history; he asked the "Supreme Judge" to decide in favor of justice, truth and right. He appealed to the "God of Battles" to fight the Negro's cause for "life, liberty and the pursuit of happiness." He implored the "Prince of Peace" to bring about the friendly relations between the two races that existed before the Civil War, when the interest of "man and master" were one. He imploringly asked the "God of Truth and Love" why it was that the two races could not get along together, as of yore. Was it because the present white folks were better than their forefathers, or was the black people of to-day worse—more dishonest and immoral than their parents of the days of bondage. He asked the "God of Heaven and Earth" to speed the day when the spirit of prejudice would disappear like the morning mist, as the sun of civilization rises towards its zenith, and men learn, with the aid of a broken education and more enlightened mental vision, that we all have a common heritage of virtues and—failings from whatever race we may be descended. He then prayed for Stratton's salvation, on this the eve of his untimely death, and ended his prayer in the good old Baptist style with: "After all our work is done here on earth, han' us down ter our co'd water graves in peace, and raise our spirrits high and happy in de kingdum is my prayer."

It was an eloquent prayer and sermon. It was delivered in the broken Negro dialect of his section. It was, however, a prayer we hope will be answered in the near future.

They arose and stood in silence for a few moments. Stratton was the first to speak: "Uncle Tom, how in the world am I to be 'handed down to a cold water grave in peace,' if they are going to burn me at the stake? Where did you get that cold water grave business?"

"Why, out of their Bible, yo' knows. Yo' kin read: yo' know where to find it in two eye John or some other part; any way I must go, so good bye my son, good bye my gal, God bless yo' both," and Uncle Tom rushed out and was soon lost in the woods.

Chapter X THE VIGILANT COMMITTEE'S DECISION

Jerry and Ella Stratton watched Uncle Tom disappear in the twilight through the woods; they then faced each other and stood in silence for two or three minutes. Ella at last broke down and burst out in tears: "Oh Jerry forgive me! Oh please forgive me for bringing you here to your death; but I will die with you—if they lynch you, they must also lynch your wife. Yes, they must lynch us both. You are the only man I ever truly loved, and a woman will go to and through hell for the man she loves. We will—"

"Keep quiet Ella until I map out some plan of escape," interrupted Stratton. "I have it; we will take everything we can carry of value and start for Charleston or some other seaport. We will be able to hire one or two horses and wagons and reach the seashore, then we can take the train together (or at least go on the same train) North until we reach Washington. I have learned that even these lawless Negro hating devils have the profound reverence and respect for the birthday of Christ. They would not dare commit murder on a holy day like Christmas or Good Friday; in the meantime as the old saying is: 'He who is fore warned is fore armed.' I will clean up my rifles and place them and the cartridges upon the table, where they will be handy in case of surprise. You can't trust these people; I have learned that fact the few days we have been here. I know one thing—"

"Oh Jerry," interrupted Ella.

"Don't interrupt me Ella, you are excited; facts are facts, and the fact of the matter is that we are in a hole and must not stop to debate which one of us got us here, but try to get out. Now there must not be any sleep to-night and at dawn we will start homeward. If we wait until the next day all will be lost, as they will, perhaps, start on their murderous mission the minute after the clock strikes midnight to-morrow and Christmas is a thing of the past until next year. Don't cry, tears will do no good in this case. You cook that wild duck I shot to-day and make some of Uncle Tom's corn bread, and we will have what may be our last supper together."

Ella started to prepare the supper while Jerry inspected, cleaned and loaded his rifles.

When Uncle Tom was praying for the white folks of the South in general, and those of his section in particular, that God would change their savage, murderous hearts to those of civilized, human and fair-minded creatures, built in the image of God, a scene was being enacted in the cross road hamlet, (the people of the community flattered it by calling it a village). It was a cross road hamlet of about fifty buildings, consisting of three stores, one cotton warehouse, a blacksmith shop, a carpenter shop, two churches and a "tavern" or hotel. The rest of the buildings were private homes of the "best families" of the county.

Captain Willoughby, the landlord of the tavern, was a little fat old man with a large bald head and sharp dishonest, though business-like eyes. He was what the natives of the community called a "foreigner," coming from New Orleans (so he said) after the close of the War of Rebellion, where he had been the captain of a Mississippi river packet that coined money before the war, bringing slaves from up the river to the New Orleans slave market. The only proof that his statement was true was that he brought with him a bag of gold with which he bought the old "Thompson tavern," which had been closed for ten years, and was slowly rotting down. He patched it up, painted it white, furnished it with second hand furniture from Charleston, thereby filling "a long felt want" in the village.

None but "the best citizens of the community" met there to drink their brandy and sugar or "hot toddy," and perfect their future plans for good or bad. Every lawless act, from the days of the Khu Klux Klan's up to the present Christmas Eve, that had been enacted in the neighborhood, was hatched out in old man Willoughby's "setting" room in the tavern. The tavern had a frontage of about sixty feet and ran back about forty feet. The "setting" room was an old fashioned tavern front room of about forty feet square, the floor of which had first been stained with elder berry juice and then oiled with cotton seed oil, giving it a dull "ox blood" red color. In the right hand corner of the room was the bar, over which Captain Willoughby presided. In the middle of the room was a fire place upon which a cheerful wood fire burned on this evening. Around this fire some were seated at the round table near it, and others were standing. Leaning against the mantle place—were seven out of the ten "best citizens of the community." They were according to ages: Dr. Tom Baxter, Lawyer Newton Capps, Mr. John Capers, Mr. Tom Marlon, Dr. James J. Bell, Mr. "Buck" Walker (the richest planters in the section) and Martin W. Sykes, a young theological student, whose father was, and grandfather had been, both ministers of the gospel of the Son of God. The grandfather having had more than a local fame, for his missionary work among the Negroes, whom he taught to fear God and obey their masters, proving (or trying to do so) that they were an inferior race, born and created bondmen for the whites.

The fortunes (or misfortune) of the Civil War, had left Martin W. Sykes a poor man of blue South Carolina blood, and in order to complete his studies for the ministry, he was obliged to earn every honest (?) penny that came his way. He was the youngest man of the seven, being only 25 years old. He had been at the Baltimore Theological College for two years and had one more year to study before he would graduate as a full-fledged minister of the teachings of Christ. Before he went to college he was the local reporter and newsgatherer for the community, and kept the wolf from the door by sending the weekly social and other events of the county to the leading newspaper at Charleston. He had also been the Charleston correspondent of the *New York Sensation*, a leading yellow journal of Greater New York City.

Dr. Tom Baxter was the "first citizen of the community." He was 72 and perfectly healthy in body and mind. He had been, in the good old days before the war, the richest slave holder and "nigger trader" in the state. He was at this time a retired physician and extensive planter and the ruler of the county; a hard task master and a hater of "niggers" and Yankees. His word was law. He was a stately old man, wore square rimmed gold spectacles, and a full beard and bushy head of hair—a mixture of deep red and gray.

Newton Capps was about 45 years old. He was the legal light of the county and the owner of one of the three stores. He was the man who fired the balls Dr. Baxter made. Dr. Bell was about 50 and was the leading physician in the section. "Buck" Walker was the leading "truck" planter, who furnished early vegetables and strawberries for the markets of New York, Boston, Philadelphia and Chicago. He always had an eye to business.

Dr. Tom Baxter, Lawyer Newton Capps and the theological student stood with their backs to the fire, while the other members of the "council of war, law and order" were seated around the table discussing the merits of a bottle of brandy and several glasses of hot "toddy." Dr. Baxter advanced to the middle of the group, took his long reed-stem red clay pipe from his mouth and standing erect with a soldierly posting, and thus addressed his associates:

"Gentlemen—We do not want to lose sight of the moral necessity of lynching that 'nigger'—burning him at the stake—in the interest of our wives and daughters. This 'nigger' comes here from the North and lives with a white woman—a native of this section, and a member of one of the oldest and most highly respected families of the state. Her grandfather, as most of us know, was a distinguished general in our great war for State Rights. This poor girl (who appears to be demented) ran away North a few years ago and was disowned by an honorable family. Under the teachings of the d— Yankees, who say that they believe a 'nigger' is as good as a white man, she has disgraced her clan by associating with a 'nigger,' and brings him down here to disgrace us. Why, this is the most bitter disgrace we have ever been subjugated to, with one exception that was during the war when a company of d—Yankee soldiers came here, took the place, slept in our beds and forced our wives and daughters to cook breakfast for them the next morning before they marched to Charleston. I say we must burn that 'nigger' at the stake, not later than day after to-morrow, as a warning to our own 'niggers' and a rebuke to the social and civil teachings of these d—Yankees we all hate in our hearts. Let me say gentlemen, I fully believe, yes know, that all loyal Southern white men will hate a Yankee and a 'nigger' for several generations hence."

These logical remarks (from a Southern white man's viewpoint) were well taken by those who heard them, and after the majority had expressed their views, which were about the same as their aged leader, it was decided to burn Stratton at the stake the night after Christmas, before the merry makers returned to their distant farms and plantations.

Martin W. Sykes, Esq., asked permission to add a few remarks, and made a timely suggestion. He deplored the action they were about to take; he called the gentleman's attention to the fact that executions or burning at the stake without trial by a jury of white men, (if not a jury of the accused peers), was in the eyes of God and the civilized world, murder; but, he added, that there were exceptions to all rules, and the present case was a grave exception. He deplored the fact that the Negro was so much inferior to the white man; that all the preachings and teachings of the superior race could not raise the poor benighted son of Africa up to the high moral standard for the white brother. He agreed with the other gentlemen that, for the good of the community, it was expedient that they burn Stratton at the stake, but that they hang old man Tom (Uncle Tom) to a neighboring tree for the part he had taken in this disgraceful affair. The only point in which he differed from the rest was that he advocated immediate action that night, and pointed to the fact that delays were dangerous. His point was well taken, and it was decided to lynch the two men that night before 12 o'clock. The several other members of the committee went out to notify the poor whites, who were to do the dirty work, while Mr. Martin W. Sykes remained at the tavern and wrote up for the *New York Morning Sensation* a full account of the lynching.

Chapter XI   THE LYNCHING BEE

Dr. Baxter went to his store, where he informed the poor whites he found assembled there, drinking his corn whiskey that a "nigger" was to be lynched—burned at the stake—down at the crossroads at midnight. He wanted them all to be there, without fail, and, of course, bring their "shooting irons." He did not tell them what crime the "nigger" had committed, and they dare not ask. To hear Dr. Tom Baxter was to obey him. Then it was of little concern to them whether the "nigger" had failed to lift his hat to Dr. Tom Baxter or had "outraged a thousand of the fair daughters of the Palmetto State."

Newton Capps and Dr. Bell went to the other store and informed the crackers that there would be a lynching that night, just before midnight. They were more considerate than Dr. Baxter, for they told their "poor white" friends that two "niggers" were to be lynched (one burned to the stake) for kidnaping a young white lady and keeping her for weeks in a log cabin, where they had subjected her to all kinds of insults and outrages the human brain could conceive. They were to meet at the old cotton warehouse at 9 o'clock for "instruction," and all promised to be there. The joyful news spread like wildfire. Some ran home to get their guns, others jumped up on the backs of mules and horses and rode out into the interior for ten miles to inform the poor whites that there was to be a "nigger" lynching. Three "Crackers" rode to the neighboring hamlet, London Bridge, seven miles away. About fifty white males averaging in age from twelve to sixty were informed that "the pleasure of their company was earnestly requested" at a "nigger" lynching, and every man and boy (after going home and getting their guns and revolvers) started on a dead run for the hamlet in which the lynching was to take place. Eight o'clock found every white male over twelve years old residing in two counties standing before the old cotton storehouse. The Negro Americans, who numbered ten to one of the white, were conspicuous by their absence.

It had been an open secret for over a week that there was going to be what the whites who had been indirectly informed called fun, and what the Negro Americans called trouble. Neither party knew the exact time the "fun" or trouble would take place, but both blacks and whites had been informed in the usual mysterious way that it would be some time after "Christmas candle light." The wise Negro Americans knew that after "candle light" meant any time after dark, and told the unwise ones so. The result was that every Negro American who was not looking for trouble (and none were) came out to the crossroad stores before noon and exchanged their eggs for "toddy" and whiskey and sugar and went home. The more frightened ones had started for Charleston. The Negro Americans of this section were not cowards, neither were they fools. In the county every male citizen over ten had been restricted from having in his house guns, pistols or other firearms when the local inspector called (after he had informed the whites a la New York city police not on dens of vice). In the next county a Negro American could not buy firearms "for love or money." These people knew that "discretion was the better part of valor," and that ten poor whites with repeating guns were brave men when they went out to kill one unarmed "nigger." Facts are facts, and this is simply (from A to Z) a romantic record of facts—a few unwritten pages in the history of "the land of the free and the home of the brave"—God's country, these United States of America. Ten o'clock found every white male over twelve years old, residing within ten square miles of the old cotton warehouse, standing "armed to the teeth" before the warehouse. Dr. Baxter sent down to his store for twenty-five candles and as many potatoes. When he got the same he and Dr. Bell entered the old ghostly warehouse, and while Dr. Bell held one lighted candle the older doctor cut a hole in the potatoes and then cut off the ends so that they would stand upon the window sills of the large gloomy interior of the old warehouse. The number of candles was not sufficient to light up the place properly and gave it a weird light.

The place was soon filled to the door with Negro blood-thirsty white men of all ages and classes, impatient and anxious to receive their last instructions from their leader, Dr. Baxter, before they rushed down the road to perform the pleasant task of lynching a "nigger" or two.

Dr. Baxter stood in the middle of the room upon a dry goods box, and several times stamped his feet and yelled "silence." At last all was still. The pencil of no artist skilled in the drawing of Satan, his imps and their infernal abode could do justice to the scene. Dr. Baxter was short and pointed. He told his followers that a "foreign nigger" had kidnapped a young white woman and had her confined in a log cabin about half a mile below the village at the crossroads. They were going to burn him at the stake, rescue the girl and put her in an asylum (as she had doubtless lost her reason since her forced confinement). The "local nigger," old Uncle Tom, who had been in the past a good, quiet, harmless darkey, was perhaps forced to harbor the "foreign nigger" against his will, or by a big offer of money. In view of his past good record the vigilance committee had decided not to burn him at the stake, but simply hang him as a warning to other weak-minded local darkies. Dr. Baxter concluded by telling them to see that their guns were loaded, but not to shoot unless so instructed by him. There was a lot of old lumber in the corner of the warehouse from which was selected several pieces of chain and rope, after which Dr. Baxter gave the word, "forward march," and the mob, now nearly three hundred strong, made a mad rush down the road towards "Uncle Tom's cabin," where we left Jerry Stratton cleaning and loading his rifles and Ella cooking the supper.

Mr. Martin W. Sykes was at that time just entering Charleston with the forewritten account of the lynching, which he at once telegraphed in full to the *New York Morning Sensation*, which also printed an evening edition, or, more properly speaking, an edition every two or three hours from daybreak to midnight.

It was just half-past 10 that night (New York City time) when the newsboys of New York rushed out of the publication office of the *New York Sensation* with copies of that paper hot from the pressroom. The streets were full of people. One bright businesslike lad, with two perfect lungs, started the cry which his companions took up (several of whom were Negro boys), and soon the air was filled with yells of "Extray! Extre-e-e! Git ther extray. Full account of the lynching and race riot down South. Great excitement in Charleston. One man shooter kill soldiers call out. Oh! get ther extray." It is the custom of New York City newsboys to run four or five words together to excite the curiosity of the passerby and make him buy a paper. The [evening papers] mentioned "sold like hot cakes." Those who bought copies read the following with large full page headlines printed in red ink:

EXTRA!!!

RACE RIOT Is Feared IN SOUTH CAROLINA!
Because Two NEGROES WERE LYNCHED
Is Feared That THE STATE TROOPS
Will Be CALLED OUT.

(From Our Special Correspondent.)
Charleston, S. C., Dec. 25.

The beautiful little village of C——, twenty miles south of this city, is in the hands of a mob of wild and excited Negroes, who threaten to murder every white person from the cradle up. As the Negroes in this section number nine to one white person, the citizens have grave fears as to the results. Dr. Thomas Baxter, the leading citizen of the community, has wired the Governor for troops, as more than five hundred armed Negroes are camped just outside of the village.

The cause of this Negro uprising was the justifiable lynching of two Negroes late this afternoon for committing an outrage upon a white girl. The facts in the case are that a strange Negro, claiming to be a Pullman car porter, residing in New York City, came to C___ a few days ago and took up his abode at the log hut of an old Negro, "Uncle Tom," who had heretofore borne a good name in the community with the best white citizen. The Northern Negro, Jerry Stratton, spent money freely with the local Negroes at the village stores, hunted on posted land, stared at white ladies, talked impudent to the leading white men of the community, and in several other minor ways made himself obnoxious to the white people. His influence over the local Negroes was soon noticed by their impudence to whites. The climax was reached a few days ago when a young white lady, the granddaughter of a distinguished Confederate general—the hero of the battle of Fort Pillow—was returning home at night fall. She was struck on the back of the head by this Northern darkey with a sandbag and dragged for half a mile to the log hut of the old Negro "Uncle Tom," where she was kept for several days beaten, starved and outraged before the facts were known to the white citizens. The old Negro, either from fear or a large bribe of money, failed to report the outrage. The fifth day as he was going to the village store she managed to pin unseen to the back of his coat a note containing the startling facts enclosed in an envelope marked: Help! Read this note! When the old Negro reached the store one of the best citizens in the community saw it, took it off and read its contents. The news spread like wildfire and this afternoon about fifty of the best citizens in the community surrounded the Negro hut, rescued the girl and burned the Negro "Jerry" at the stake. The young lady struck the match herself, and set fire to the light wood which slowly consumed the black wretch. The old Negro confessed all and in view of his past good record was simply hanged to a neighboring tree his body riddled with buckshot and left hanging with a warning to all the local darkies nailed on to his breast on a placard:

NIGGERS
TAKE
WARNING

The Negroes are arming for revenge and have surrounded the town several hundred strong. It is reported that they have burned several barns and cotton gins and killed three white children a few miles above C——. Great excitement prevails. Dr. Thomas Baxter, mayor of the town, has sent a telegram to the Governor asking for troops to protect the law-abiding white citizens.

Mr. Martin W. Sykes was not sending this dispatch (which he believed was true, in the main, to-wit, that Jerry Stratton had been burned at the stake and Uncle Tom strung up to a tree) "for his health." He kept in communication with the *New York Sensation* until he received a telegraphic money order, and then after some changes and improvements, sold his story to the Charleston agency of the Associated Press in time for it to appear in every morning newspaper of note in the United States on the morning of the 26th. Many of the

New York City papers had editorials upon the lynching, and most of these editorials justified the lynching. The few white friends of the Negro, of the good old Charles Sumner stripe, were discouraged and downhearted. The majority of New York City's white population said "it was right," and they would have done the same thing (even in New York) if it had been a female relative of theirs.

We know that more than half of Sykes' story was false. Let us return to South Carolina and see how much of it was true.

Chapter XII   THE ESCAPE

The mob of lynchers rushed down the road towards "Uncle Tom's" cabin. When within a few hundred yards of the cabin, above a bend in the road, with pine woods on either side, the mob gave a yell—the yell all old G.A.R. men who fought on land in the Civil War will recall.

"Silence! D— you. Silence! Do you want to arouse the niggers and give them an opportunity to escape their just punishment? No more of those yells. March silently until you reach the other side of the bend in the road, then about twenty-five of you go across fields to the right and twenty five to the left, and surround the house. When the rest of us reach there knock on the door, and when it is opened pull the niggers out, or if they do not open the door break it in," remarked Dr. Tom Baxter.

The warning came too late. Jerry Stratton heard the rebel yell break out upon the silent midnight air, and remarked to Ella:

"Here they come; put out the lights and do not speak." He was a good marksman, and selected the best of his repeating rifles and calmly cleaned the range glass on the barrel of the gun. "I know these Southern gents outnumber me a couple of hundred to one and will kill me in the end, but as I have committed no crime (except coming down here) I am going to sell my life as dearly as I can," remarked Stratton as the mob turned around the curve of the road. The full moon was at its zenith, making the night as bright as day.

The mob, the size of a small army, moved forward, with Newton Capps, "Buck" Walker, Dr. James Bell and Dr. Tom Baxter in the lead. They stopped in the open road, just outside of the range of Jerry Stratton's repeating rifle. Dr. Tom Baxter pointed the way on each side of the road to the fifty odd men who were to go around about way and surround the house. They advanced. Stratton, with his rifle at his shoulder, sighted them until they were over twenty-five feet within the range of his gun, then he drew a bee line on the first man to the right, Newton Capps, and fired. Bang! Bang! Bang! and three men, Capps, Walker and Dr. Bell, fell to the earth. Dr. Baxter, hearing the shots, and seeing the men fall dead, rightly concluded that the fourth shot would kill him, and he fell a second after the third shot, just before the fourth. The fourth shot struck a man in the next rank in the shoulder, and he dropped down in fear. Stratton had never studied the art of science of war, but it came to him in a minute after the front rank fell, to shoot low and cripple his foes, as it would take two men to take one injured from the field of battle. He fired about twenty-five shots, all but one hitting a mark. These shots caused a retreat—a stampede—of the mob. Someone yelled, "The house is full of niggers all armed. Here they come." The mob rushed backward, their brave leader, Dr. Baxter, in the lead. After they had retreated around the bend in the road, behind the woods, Dr. Tom

Baxter regained his courage and thus addressed them: "Boys, that house is full of armed niggers, but we will get them out. Three of you men get into this cart and drive over to my house; in my barn you will find three small cannon we used in the war with the Yankees. I have balls and powder at the store, bring the cannon here and we will plant it at the curve and blow the niggers sky high. We will be beyond their range."

Three men started for the cannon, and the rest of the mob went in the old cotton warehouse and waited. When Jerry Stratton saw them retreat, he reached a conclusion. "Hurry up, Ella, and let us pack up and get out, the cowards have gone for more men. They concluded that two hundred (minus those I have killed) were not enough to kill one 'nigger,' and have gone for more brave men," he remarked as he refilled his rifles.

"Hurry up, Ella; pack up all of your things that you can comfortably carry, disguise yourself by putting on a suit of mine, and let us get out. We have no time to lose." Ella did as she was directed without any comment pro or con, a remarkable thing for any woman to do. When they were prepared to leave the cabin Jerry got some flour and rubbed over his face; he then pulled a hunting cap down almost over his eyes and turned his coat collar up. The greater part of his face was hid, and what was exposed looked white from the flour. Ella, with a duck hunting suit, looked like a man instead of a woman, and armed with a rifle each, they prepared to leave the cabin. Jerry took a can of oil and poured it over the floor and sides of the house. He went out in the barn and brought in a keg of turpentine, which he also poured over the floor.

"What are you going to do?" asked Ella.

"Why, set the house on fire, of course. When they see the house burning, they will conclude that some of the braver of their men have stolen up and set the house on fire and burned us up. This will throw them off our track, and prevent them following us."

He raked the hot wood coals out of the fire into the middle of the floor. "Good bye 'Uncle Tom's Cabin,' and good bye (we hope) old Palmetto State," he remarked as he and Ella rushed from the burning house. They stood a few hundred yards down the road to the southward (the same way Uncle Tom had gone). All nature seemed to favor the Strattons in their fight for life. When the attack was made upon them, the full moon made the midnight as bright as day, which aided Jerry to shoot a few of the best citizens of the community. Now, as they took their flight northward, the moon was hidden behind black clouds, and the night was dark. Dressed like two city hunters, they hurried down the road towards Charleston, miles away.

When the house was all of a blaze, Dr. Tom Baxter saw the reflection upon the midnight sky. "The hut's afire. Some of our boys have stolen up and set it afire. Let us hurry down and see the niggers roast," he yelled, as he led the wild mob on a run down the road. When they had turned the bend in the road and were in full view of the burning cottage log cabin, they all stopped. Some one with enough imagination to be a writer of romance yelled, "See them! See them dancing about in the fire? See the girl! Shall we try and save her?"

"No!" yelled Dr. Baxter. "Let her burn with the niggers. Advance and fire at the house, so if any of them get out they will be shot." Immediately about one hundred shots were fired at the burning house. In the meantime the cannon arrived upon the field of battle and was placed in position, loaded and fired several times at the burning log cabin. The fire at last burned out and Dr. Baxter concluded that the "niggers" were all dead, and the party returned to the village. They stumbled over the dead bodies of their brave comrades. Dr. Baxter waved silence. "Pick up those bodies and put them in the cart and take them to the old cotton warehouse," he said to the men nearest to the dead lynchers. They obeyed in silence. "Now, boys," continued the doctor, "we don't want the outside world to know that those niggers killed three white men. We have no telegraph from here to Charleston, and the rest of the world will never know it unless some one here tells it, and the man who does will die like a dog. Remember!"

The outside world has never known until now how three of the best citizens of C——met an untimely death at the hands of a Negro fighting for his life. Their friends and relatives were told by Dr. Baxter that they were accidentally shot in a deer hunt and so it is recorded.

When Jerry and Ella Stratton had gone about two miles down the road, they met a country cart with two youths about sixteen. They were driving in a hurry, but stopped to ask the huntsmen how far it was to C——, as they were going to a nigger lynching.

"You are too late boys. It is all over. We have just come from there, but if you want to make a dollar each, turn your horse around and drive us in to Charleston or near there. We must be there by daybreak on business of importance. What do you say?"

The boys accepted the terms and drove Jerry and Ella within a half mile of Charleston to the Negro settlement of Lincolnville, where they hired a "hack" and started for the city. During the ride

Stratton jumped from the coach and went on foot to the dock of the New York and Charleston Steamship Company, where he engaged steerage passage to New York City. A few hours before the steamer sailed a white lady dressed as a widow secured a first-class stateroom. The good ship sailed. A few days later, as they landed in New York City, Jerry Stratton sang:

> Home again, home again;
> Home from a foreign shore;
> Oh, how it fills my heart with joy
> To be at home once more.

Chapter XIII   THE SEPARATION

The scare Jerry and Ella Stratton got from their visit to the "New South" made an impression on them for about one month, during which time they lived a quiet, respectable life as "Mr. and Mrs. J. W. Brown." It is hard for "sporting" people to reform in New York City; the temptations are too great, and the Strattons soon drifted back into their fast life. Ella, in fact, tried to make up for lost time. She drank and smoked more. As a result in one year, she looked ten years older. One day, under the influence of liquor, in getting off a car, she fell in the street and was taken to St. Vincent's Hospital in an unconscious state with a cut head. She was out of her mind for two weeks. The account of her falling on the street and being taken to St. Vincent's Hospital appeared in all of the morning papers, and Jerry at once hastened to the hospital to see her. He had fore-thought enough to say that he had a message from her husband which he wanted to deliver in person. The hospital doctors decided it would not be prudent to show the letter at this time, no matter what the contents might be. They therefore filed it for her reading when she was ready to leave the hospital. Jerry Stratton called every morning for ten days, and when he was refused admittance to the bedside of his sick wife, he went away and wrote her a letter each day. These letters the hospital people filed away and did not give them to her. At last Jerry Stratton concluded that it was a dodge of Ella's to get rid of him, and employed a private white detective to investigate the case. This fellow, who was of Southern birth, after hearing Stratton's story in full, took his money, but never went near the hospital. He reported to Stratton that he had investigated the matter, and found out that Ella was not sick, but employed there as a nurse; that she did not care to see him—in fact, she was tired of him, and wanted to get rid of him, and had taken heroic steps to do so. Jerry Stratton believed the detective's lie, and wrote her the following farewell letter:

No.— W. 333rd St., New York City.

June 16, 18—

Dear Ella—I have called several times to see you at the hospital. Each time I have been told by a doctor or an attendant that you could not be seen. Each day I wrote a letter [inquiring] about your health and everything, and have received no reply.

I have positive and well known reasons to know that you are not an inmate of the hospital, but employed there as a trained nurse; that you have (woman like) got tired of your dark-brown top; that you have reflected and have resolved to reform (at least in regards to me). I have in mind an old song, a part of which runs this way

> Take her, you are welcome,
> But you soon will find it true
> That she who can be false to one
> Can be the same to two.

To which I will fondly and respectfully add that the woman who can be false to two men of her race can hardly be expected—in fact, can not be expected—to be true to one of the other race. However, Ella, I was foolish enough to conclude, after our down South experience, and the heroic stand you took, that you did love me, and when we again set our feet upon the soil of God's country, we would live together as happily as people in our set, and that you would be as true to me as, well—women of your set. It was all a dream. Yes.

> We are parted from each other,
> And our dream of love is past,
> The bright dream was too beautiful
> to last

If I do not hear from you in three days, you will never see or hear from me again, and you will be able to conclude without the aid of a doctor, lawyer, judge or jury, my opinion in future of women in general, regardless of their race, color or previous condition.

Jerry Stratton

About two weeks after this letter was received at the hospital, Ella was pronounced cured of all traces of liquor or cigarette smoking. She had when found a large sum of money, which the hospital people kept for her and returned with the letters of Jerry Stratton a few minutes before she left. She paid all bills due and rewarded the nurses who had attended her. As she started to leave, the letters still in her hand unopened, she remarked to the head physician, Dr. Cross: "Good bye, doctor: I am under lasting obligations to you and all connected with the hospital. You have made a new woman of me physically, mentally, morally and—I am, in fact, almost persuaded to become a Catholic" (the St. Vincent Hospital was a Catholic institution). "Any way," she continued, "I am going to live a purer and better life in the future, and hope when I die that the world will be a small degree better for my having lived in it. Good morning."

She turned to go, when the doctor called her attention to the unopened letters in her hand. After thanking him, she sat down at the table in the reception room and looked at the half score of letters. She at once saw that the handwriting was that of Jerry Stratton. She looked at the postmarks and placed them one by one in a row, according to the dates. She then read them carefully. She then turned to the doctor and said in an angry, excited tone: "Why have you people kept these letters from me so long. I have been in a condition to read newspapers for the past three weeks. Was it because you knew from whom they came? I learn by these letters that several drop letters have been left here for me. Where are they? What right have you to pry into an inmate's private business?" Without waiting for an answer from the surprised doctor, she rushed out and hurried to the nearest telephone station, where she telephoned for a cab and directed the driver to take her to the flat she and Jerry Stratton occupied the day of the accident.

Here she learned that he had left there several weeks prior, but left a note with the janitor for her, in which, he said she would find all of their furniture and other goods in the Eagle storage house, rent for the same paid for one year, with agreement for rebate whenever taken out before the end of the year. The note also stated that long before she received it, he would be dead to the New York City sporting world "for the present," and to her "forever and a day" and that he wished her well. The note ended with, in the language of Lord Byron:

> Fare thee well, and—If forever,
> Still, forever, fare thee well
>
> *Jerry Stratton.*

Chapter XIV   HER ATONEMENT

Ella Stratton was a thrice changed woman after she had tried, with the aid of several private detectives, to find Jerry, without success. She knew that he was alive and in some unknown part of the world (or perhaps the United States) laboring under the impression that she had been false to him. She resolved to atone for her past wild acts; she resolved to live a purer and better life; she resolved to do all in her power to better the condition of the poor colored people of Greater New York. Meeting so many old companions who tried to lead her back into the old paths of pleasure and vice, she removed to Brooklyn, where she was unknown, and took board with an old German couple under her maiden name, Ella Forrester. During the day she would walk around in the several sections of Brooklyn where Negro Americans resided and buy food, coal and wood for those she concluded were worthy objects of charity.

One morning she went down town on Fulton Street, in the dry goods district, to make some purchases for herself. As she was about to go up the steps of the elevated railroad station, she felt a heavy hand pull her back. Looking around, her eyes met those of old Captain Seabergh.

"My dear girl, I love you still. Yes, still, although you 'done' me on the train between here and Chicago. You"—

"Unhand me, sir," broke in Ella.

"Oh, I see you are on the stage now. You are an actress. You are, perhaps, the leading lady in some ten-cent play. I will 'unhand' you, as you request me, but I must speak with you, no matter how painful it is to you."

Ella broke away from him and entered the next car. He followed her, but was prudent enough to sit unobserved by her in a corner opposite. When she left the car, he followed her to her home, or, more properly speaking, her rooms, and entered before she could object.

He threw a check for $10,000 on the table and also placed a roll of $600 in bills on the table. "There, little girl, is your part of my will. I don't believe I will live much longer."

Ella stood up and pointed first to the money and then to the door. "Take back your gold, for [you] will never buy me," she said in a stage whisper.

"Oh!" said the old man, as he took up his check and money, and started to depart, "I will see you again when you are either sober or in hard luck."

Six months later a man called upon Ella at her home; he was Captain Seabergh's lawyer; he informed her that Captain Seabergh was dead—had been run over by a trolley car, that a roll of bills, minus his commission, were hers. The total sum was over nine thousand dollars in cold cash or at least bills (greenbacks and brown backs of small denomination of twenty and fifty dollar bills). The lawyer was gone—the money was there. "I will make this a 'conscience fund' and build a home and mission for needy colored people and name it after my husband, 'Jerry Stratton,'" she said to herself.

In the section of Brooklyn, locally known as "New Brooklyn" is a subsection that, fifty years ago, was owned by Negroes and known as "Weeksville." At the time of the date of our story, there were more colored people in this section than any part of the late "City of Churches." The bad and worthy poor colored people, as well as the good and well-to-do, resided in this section; "Chicago Row," who in "Greater New York" has not heard of the infamous and immoral "Chicago Row?" "Chicago Row" has a history; it was not always "Chicago Row." About twenty-five years before our opening, a German bought a half "block" (or square) of lots, upon which he built a row of houses, which he rented to white people. The house above was also owned by a German, who rented it to a Negro woman of questionable bearings. One by one their places were filled by the lowest Negroes in Greater New York. Chicago Row soon became the home of the lowest Negroes in the section, who were inter-larded with poor respectable colored people, who took advantage of the cheap rent. The "Row" spread all over the south side of the block (or square) and then across the street, until the whole block (or square) was composed of Negroes. The vacant lots fell in value. When Ella tried to buy two lots of fifty feet frontage, they were sold to her for a song. She built a mission and home for colored people which she called "The Jerry Stratton Mission and Home for Aged Colored People." In the chapel there was a memorial tablet dedicated to the late Jerry Stratton and a life-size crayon picture of him behind the altar. It was the night before Christmas ten years after the date of our opening chapter. The worthy colored poor had been told to call at the mission that night when they would receive a well-filled basket containing all the parts of a Greater New York Christmas dinner, and hundreds took advantage of the opportunity. Their donor's heart was made glad, and the "good white lady," as the community called the reformed Ella, received their blessings.

During the winter months she gave each day portions of food and fuel to the worthy colored poor, and, and as it is often hard to distinguish between the just and the unjust, the good and the bad or the worthy and the unworthy, many a good-for-nothing Chicago Row loafer lived in clover for years. During the week she had kindergartens for the little children, where she taught them to sew and make themselves useful, clean, and neat. At night she had prayer meetings and lectures. She greatly improved the condition of the worthy poor and had some redeeming influence over the lower class of Negroes.

She still remained a mystery to the colored people in general, and the community and city in particular. She was only known as "Miss Ella," and all the children (and some of the aged inmates of the home) declared that she had no other name than that of "Miss Ella."

There were two newspaper men—one black, the other white—who resolved to solve the mystery of "Miss Ella's" past life. To one—the colored man—it was promotion to the staff of his paper; to the other it was cold cash. They searched the records and found out that the property was duly recorded and the trustees of the institution were some of the leading citizens of Brooklyn. The record also stated that the founder was a "Miss Ella Hope."

The colored reporter got the inside track, drew largely upon his imagination (as all Greater New York newspaper men—the author excepted—do) and wrote for the *Brooklyn Eagle* the following:

—————— A NOBLE CHARITY. ——————

The Jerry Stratton Mission and Home for Aged Colored People, situated on Atlantic Avenue, near Troy Avenue, in the section of Brooklyn where the most needy (and candor compels us to say), [and] most depraved colored people resided is a worthy and lasting monument to a noble and benevolent Christian lady, who has the good work under her careful eye, in the person of Miss Ella Hope. The estate has a frontage on Atlantic Avenue of three hundred feet and runs back two hundred feet, upon which are several buildings, the largest being the Old Folks Home, which is five stories high and built in the form of a Greek cross, at a cost of several thousand dollars. Here all worthy aged colored homeless or poor people can find an asylum the rest of their reclining years.

Miss Ella Hope comes from old Abolitionist stock. Her grandfather, General Seth Hope, was one of the Quaker pioneers of Brattleboro, Vermont, where Miss Hope was born fifty-five years ago. Her father was a personal friend of the great Abolitionist, John Brown, and was with him at Harper's Ferry.

When the reporter called yesterday he was shown all over the several buildings by Miss Hope, whose pious face, snow-white locks, kindly, beaming eyes and friendly hand convinced him that this warm-hearted lady was the right person in the right place. At present the institution is in need of a little outside help, and philanthropic people in general and friends of the colored people in particular would do well to send Miss Hope a check so the good work she has started may continue.

Ella did not see the article, and was greatly surprised when she received several goodly checks for the institution.

In looking over his exchanges the Sunday editor of the *New York Recorder* saw the article in the *Eagle* and concluded to write up the institution. He sent a snap-shot man to take pictures of the buildings and a smart young reporter to write it up. After they had taken several pictures of the buildings, the reporter entered, pencil and pad in hand, and commenced to interview Ella. She was surprised and refused to answer his pointed questions. He showed her the article in the "Eagle," which she read carefully with an amused smile upon her face. When she had finished, she handed him back the clipping without any comment and started for the door; he remained seated, looking about the room writing. This angered her and she remarked:

"My time is of value if yours is not, sir."

"Well, as I told you, I have come to write up the institution and your life."

"I am not looking for newspaper notoriety, and if I were, I would not seek it in the columns of the *New York Recorder*, but"— she concluded, as she took a seat near him—"if you will not interrupt me with questions, I will give a short history of my life and what will in the future be my life work.

"I have lived all my life among colored people, I have studied their ways, their good points and their short comings, and have rightly concluded that they are no better or worse than white people. Among them can be found the good and the bad, the just and the unjust, the rich and the poor, the educated and the ignorant, the wise and the simple. The fact that they were born black instead of white was no fault of theirs, but an accident of birth, beyond their control (the same as yours or mine). They did not come here of their own free will, like the whites, but were stolen and taken by force from their sunny African home and brought here as slaves. Since their freedom all kinds of barriers have been placed in their progressive march to a better civilization by the whites. In the North the stores and trade unions' doors are closed against them; in the South everything, even life, liberty, and the pursuit of happiness, are denied them; still, in the face of all these barriers, the advancement they have made in the past few years has no equal upon the pages of history. Their treatment by a nation claiming to be one of the leading civilized ones of the progressive era is a blot upon the pages of the history of our beloved country.

"The colored people have advanced in every progressive road of life that the white man has trod; they have their eminent divines, their physicians, their lawyers, their teachers, their merchants and their farmers—in fact they have made, according to their small population and average, under untold difficulties, the advancement the whites have made, taking a ratio of the white and black population of the country.

"If they had not been hedged about by a wall of race prejudice, they would have outstripped the whites. My life work is to elevate and improve the condition of the colored people of Brooklyn. Why I have been so moved to do [so] is no business of the *New York Recorder* and I demand it not try to pry into my private matters. This institution is duly incorporated and recorded—the desired information not given by me can be found in the public records at City Hall—good morning," and she politely pointed the reporter the way to the door.

About ten or twelve days after Ella "Hope" (as she is now recorded) gave her Christmas dinner and well filled baskets to the poor of "Chicago Row," the *New York Recorder* published the following upon its editorial page:

A STRANGE COINCIDENCE

That the world is growing better and brighter; that man's inhumanity to man is growing less as the sun of civilization gets nearer and nearer its zenith, can be seen on all sides without the aid of field glasses; still, the door of charity is often opened by strange hands, as the clipping below from one of our far Western exchanges will show:

[From the Oakland (Cal.) Times]

Three Hundred homeless or poor men and boys of this city were given a Christmas dinner between the hours of 12:30 and 6:00 p.m. at the hotel and restaurant of Mr. Amos B. Clark, on Railroad avenue, opposite the Grand depot. Mr. Clark is one of our few colored citizens and one of our leading business men and richest property owners. He came here from Chicago several years ago (where, he says, he was born, and with strange foresight bought up all of the then worthless land west of the new Grand depot. He graded the same, built a hotel opposite the depot and built flats upon the rest of his land. These houses are all rented to worthy white people, as there are only twenty colored men residing in the city, all employees in the houses of the rich.) The strangest fact about Mr. Clark's dinner was that all of it's partakers were white, as there is not a Negro beggar or tramp in the city. Men of Mr. Clark's stripe are a credit to the State, and the Pacific slope, regardless of the hue of their skin, and we hope that Mr. Clark (who, we learn, is a bachelor and worth over $400,000) will continue to be one of our foremost charitable citizens for years, but not as a bachelor, but a benedict.

The strange coincident in the above is that at that time or near about (allowing for the difference between New York and California time) a white lady was doing the same kindly deed for the worthy Negroes of Brooklyn. The coincident points the way to a brighter future, when all Americans regardless of race, color, or other accidents of birth or misfortune will bask alike in the noon-day sun of a "country of the people, by the people, for the people." God speed the day.

|||||||||||||||||||||||||||||||||||||||||||||||||||||||||||||||||||||||||||||||||||||||||||||||||||||||||||||||||||||

The following summer a colored Pullman palace car porter stopped at Amos B. Clark's hotel. He was a stranger; he was talkative. He said he was from New York City and a native of the place. When Clark heard this, he confessed that he was also a native of the great city, and asked many questions about the places and the changes during the past few years. He also asked his guest if he had any New York or Brooklyn newspapers, no matter how old, as news from home was always new news.

The porter told him that he had only a few old papers (mostly Brooklyn ones) wrapped around some packages in his room on the car, across the street, but he would run over and get them. He did so, and gave Clark a bundle of papers about six months' old. As he handed them to Clark he looked into his face and through his full beard, and exclaimed, "As I live! it's Jerry Stratton! Why, Jerry, don't you know me, Ike Randolph? How came you here? How—" The whistle of his train blew and he was obliged to run out before he finished his questions or [heard] the answers to the same.

When he was gone Jerry Stratton (Amos B. Clark was no other) carefully read the papers, which were thick with the history pictures and the like of "Ella Hope" and the Jerry Stratton Mission and Old Colored Folks Home. He read them thrice and, as he put them in a pigeon hole in his safe, he remarked to himself, like the stoic he had grown to be, "Her atonement."

IT CAME TO PASS:
A CHRISTMAS STORY
Bruce L. Reynolds

Except for the years he wrote for the *Chicago Defender*, little is known about Bruce L. Reynolds. His career as a short story writer and columnist for the *Defender* began in 1935 and ended in 1945. His writings, published in the newspaper's national edition, were widely read. During the Great Depression, Reynolds wrote weekly stories that focused on the everyday issues African Americans were grappling with. In the early 1940s, he ceased writing short stories and became the newspaper's national "Church Editor," a position he held until 1945.

"It Came to Pass" is a traditional Christmas story that reinforces the power of religious faith, a religious cornerstone in African American history and culture. In the words of the apostle Paul, "Faith is the substance of things hoped for, the evidence of things not seen." It is a belief that God's power is infinite. In this story, Edward and Ella, an elderly couple beset by poverty, lacking food, and unable to obtain decent medical care, share a deep love for each other and an abiding faith in God.

The story opens on Christmas Eve in a large northern city whose public spaces reflect the beauty and benevolence of Christmas frequently seen in the business sections of large urban centers. Reynolds juxtaposes the opulence reflected in the private and public celebratory displays of Christmas with the abject poverty and suffering of people like Edward and Ella. He demonstrates that there are two worlds: one highly visible world of privilege and one obscure world of despair and suffering.

In 1939, during a time when the world was beset by war and America was wracked by the Great Depression, it appeared that many people had forgotten God. Reynolds reminds the reader that God is real and that he answers prayers. Arriving in the guise of a doctor, Dr. Wayne, God heals Ella and reminds Edward that all things are possible if you "just keep faith in your heart, nourish it, cherish it until it reflects in your thinking and dreaming and doing."

Edward and Ella represent the deep and transcending faith of African Americans, who survived the holocaust of the Middle Passage; the horrors of slavery; the unremitting struggle to survive poverty, lynching, and mental and physical abuse; and who fervently believed that God would also see them through the Depression. During a time of great poverty and despair, Reynolds reinforced the message of faith and hope in God.

It Came to Pass

I t was Christmas Eve. The city was covered with a fresh blanket of crunchy, white snow, and more was falling. Christmas wreaths hung in windows and on doors. Passersby could glimpse many a brightly-kited and tinsled tree. In the public park was a Christmas tree that dwarfed the humans who clustered around its base, singing carols. In the metropolitan section, a skyscraper office building had formed a striking cross with lighted windows. The clamor of church bells mingled with the stately, beautiful melody of "Silent Night, Holy Night," as played on a giant carillon in a nearby university. Hearts, unfeeling throughout a rather hectic year, were bursting with good will and good cheer and gratitude.

But it was another story in two bare, chilly basement rooms. In one of the rooms and ill [in] a bed, lay an old lady. Her suffering had pulled in her cheeks, and her eyes were like burning coals deep in two dark wells. At her bedside sat an elderly man in tattered clothes. He squinted through oval shaped glasses at an open Bible on his knees. And now he turned his eyes to the still face of his wife of nearly forty-two years.

"I can't read any more, Ella," he told her wearily. He closed the Bible disconsolately. "With so much going on in the world—war and the like—seems like we've slipped God's mind. I'm not blaming anybody or anything, Ella. But when I think of all the money spent for tomorrow, I get a little shaky knowing we have about a dollar. Of course, we'll get our basket tomorrow. Goodness knows I'm grateful for kind hearted folks. But you won't be able to eat anything, Ella. It'll be the first time we have not eaten together on Christmas."

Ella turned her head slowly to face him. "I'm sorry to spoil things, Edward." Her voice was just a whisper. "But I can't seem to hold a thing on my stomach."

"If you only had decent medical treatment," old Edward muttered. "The city doctor is all right. But he admits there isn't much he can do. Besides, he has so many calls to make, he can't take up much time with any one patient. Oh, Ella, if we could only get that specialist, Dr. Wayne, to come out. I know he could do something. The city doctor said he could. He's the best in the city."

Ella closed her eyes. "But he's a rich doctor. They say he charges five dollars a visit. He has no time for poverty stricken old folks like us. You called him twice. Each time he flatly refused to see me."

"Yes. He told us to see the city doctor."

There was a knock on the door. Edward looked quizzically at his wife.

"Wonder who that is?"

"Maybe it's that nice couple down the street, Edward."

He went to the door and opened it. A man stood smiling. He carried a small bag in one hand.

"You've been trying to contact Dr. Wayne," the man said, coming in. He opened his coat to shake off the snow. "I have come. Where is the patient?"

Old Edward fell upon his knees at the man's feet. "Thank God you've come, Dr. Wayne. Everybody seems to think you can do what others can't." He rose. "Let me help you out of your coat." He touched the doctor's arm.

Dr. Wayne shook his head. "That won't be necessary."

Old Edward jerked his hand back as though he had touched a live wire. For a moment he stared incredulously into the doctor's eyes. The uncertain light from a lamp fell across the doctor's face, revealing that his eyes were his most singular feature. They baffled description. They were not like eyes, it seemed. Rather, more like windows, across which a veil had been drawn.

"You wait here," Dr. Wayne told the old man. He went into Ella's room and closed the door.

Edward sat down and waited. That look of incredulity was still on his face. What manner of man was this Dr. Wayne? He had no sense of time. But he got to his feet when the doctor came out of Ella's room.

"Your wife wants to see you," he said. "Don't worry about tomorrow. She will be able to eat with you."

"How did you know—"

"Just keep faith in your heart. Nourish it, cherish it until it reflects in your thinking and dreaming and doing."

"What a strange thing for a doctor to say," Edward murmured.

"But not strange for me," the doctor said. "And now I must be going. Merry Christmas to you."

With that, he opened the door and was gone. Edward looked down at the steps leading out of his basement rooms. He blinked his eyes hard. Grass seemed to be growing out of the doctor's footsteps in the snow! Edward closed the door and hurried to his wife's side. He found her sitting up in bed, reading the Bible. She had not been able to sit up in bed for three months! He fell upon his knees by the bed.

"Ella—Ella, who was that?"

She smiled at him. "What does your heart tell you? You saw his eyes, Edward. You see me now."

"I touched his arm, Ella," he remembered. "I saw grass growing in the snow where he walked. Ella—"

Some carolers were singing outside. It was "Joy To The World." Understanding dawned upon Edward. His eyes filled as he found Ella's hand. Their faces were radiant. Their eyes met in mutual and glorious acknowledgment.

"He came to our bare rooms to give us the greatest Christmas gift of all."

"Yes, Edward. But remember, he was born in a manger."

A CHRISTMAS JOURNEY
Louis Lorenzo Redding

Louis Lorenzo Redding was born in Alexandria, Virginia, in 1901 and grew up in Wilmington, Delaware. In 1923, he received an undergraduate degree from Brown University and subsequently taught English at Morehouse College, in Atlanta. At the time he wrote "A Christmas Journey," he was a student at Harvard University Law School. Among the first of his race to graduate from the law school, in 1929, Redding became the first African American admitted to the bar in Delaware. Beginning as an attorney in private practice, Redding later worked with the NAACP Legal Defense and Educational Fund and as a public defender in Wilmington.

In 1950, Redding, a pioneer in the fight for the desegregation of schools and housing, represented nine African American students at Delaware State College denied admission to the all-white University of Delaware. Pursing this case, he won two landmark decisions, *Parker v. University of Delaware* and *Bulah/Belton v. Gebhart*, which provided the legal basis for desegregation in Delaware. These decisions were forerunners of the famous *Brown v. Board of Education of Topeka* case, which led to the desegregation of the nation's public schools, and they also served as catalysts for legislation ending segregation and discrimination in housing, voting, public transportation, and public facilities.

Redding's life and work were motivated by the belief that the best way to achieve racial equality was through the passage of laws. In "A Christmas Journey," he uses social realism to explore the meaning of Christmas for the dispossessed. Published in *Opportunity* in December 1925, the story reflects the pessimism and chaos that was so evident in the period following World War I. Redding employs the Christmas theme to bring attention to societal ills that he felt needed to be addressed.

Set in Boston, "A Christmas Journey" is the story of Jim and Elsie, whose lives have been led in the margins of mainstream society. Jim, a white man, is described as an incurable consumptive who knows that death is near. He believes that his condition resulted from being gassed while serving as a soldier in World War I. Elsie is a light-complexioned African American woman who is passing for white. These two characters are bonded by their love in a common-law marriage. Through the story of their lives and their personal reflections, Redding explores social issues such as interracial marriage, the social impact of tuberculosis, and society's indifference to human suffering.

Redding forces the reader to reflect upon the real meaning of Christmas: loving, sharing, and caring for others. He suggests that, for many people, Christmas has become merely another holiday in which to engage in consumerism. Although Redding demonstrates the callousness and lack of concern that can seem to permeate the Christmas celebration in a large urban center, he overlooks several central themes that have fueled mankind's existence for centuries and which force us to reflect on the meaning of Christmas and life. Christmas in the best of traditions represents a rebirth of life. It holds out the possibility for change. It stresses faith, hope, and love. Jim and Elsie, feeling disconnected from society, embrace the cynicism of the time and abandon their faith and hope. In the end, they are left with only their love for one another.

A Christmas Journey

> For Love the master symphonist
> Ignoring [vanity], creed and hue,
> Mocks dicta that stifle and twist
> To give consonant souls their due.

The raw sting of the cold, night air struck the consumptive's [shrunken] chest. He gasped, coughed, gasped again, and with a slender hand, quivering from the exertion of his coughing, drew up the collar of his overcoat.

"This thing's got me all right! That fool of an army doctor! A lot he knew about gas! And he told me that I'd wear it off in a few months! Wear it off! Well, it'll soon be off now—but not in the way he said."

Abstractedly he had taken his habitual route homeward. It led through the street market, which was thronged with Christmas-eve buyers, stocking up for the season that the morrow would usher in. The air was full of shrill babel and of the fresh smell of raw foodstuffs; the street was a jumble of motley wares. Nowhere else in great Boston could be found more eloquent proof of the cosmopolitanism of the city. Improvised signs in Yiddish, Italian, and Spanish, as well as in English, leered at the purchasers from all angles. Creeping, pipe-puffing Chinese with American overcoats over their loose native jackets bought greens from Italian merchants. Buxom Irish housewives bought red meat from German butchers. Greeks, Negroes, Poles—everybody, bought a great variety of things from that ubiquitous merchant, the Jew. Peanuts and cabbages, carrots and shoestrings, turkeys and bandannas, trousers and cheap jewelry, silk stockings and codfish—all were bargained for with equal gusto. Here, verily, was a paradise for the poor; but despite the low prices, no sale was complete without haggling.

The consumptive, as he weakly jostled his way through the alien melange, saw nothing that interested him. He was more than sated with the world. He loathed everything, even the scrawny, yellow fowl that a red-bearded Jew was swinging in the air and offering for sale in a rasping falsetto. Nor did he mask his contemptuous feelings under a hypocritical look of complacency; his wan countenance was frankly sardonic.

"Fools," he muttered between coughs, "poor, ignorant fools, to whom life is a dollar, a loaf of hard bread, an imitation diamond, and a suit of shoddy, woolen underwear! Preparing to celebrate Christmas! Bah! What do they know about Christmas—or what do they care? It's just another holiday for them!"

A heavy foreign sounding voice sang out:

"Dancin' monkeys here, only a quarter. Git a dancin' monkey."

The words shattered the cynical musings of the consumptive and sent a train of incoherent and confused images swirling through his brain.

"Dancin' monkeys——"

The sound came with haunting urgency and the man moved toward the spot from which it seemed to come. He beheld a short, unkempt, alien seeming peddler standing at the edge of the curb. On the ground beside him was a huge basket filled with bits of painted metal. In one hand the peddler held a string from the end of which dangled a monkey, crudely fashioned in tin, with a red coat and black trousers painted on his body in burlesque of the apparel of man. While the peddler lustily proclaimed his toy, he pulled the string and the monkey hopped and jumped, spun and danced. Occasionally a passer-by ventured from the main current of the crowd to look and pass on, but rarely to buy. There was no fascination for the consumptive in the terpsichorean efforts of the monkey, but he did find himself interested in the degree of imbecility that could cause anyone to invest money in such a glittering, senseless bauble. He looked at the bawling vendor with a feeling of contempt not unmixed with pity. "Why doesn't he get a real job? Anything would be more profitable than this."

But there was no answer in the loud cry of the peddler. . . . Again the emaciated man looked at the dangling monkey. He noted its gaudy, man-like costume; he watched its poor pantomime of human dancing; and he looked again at the man who held the string. The latter's eyes were bright with a far-seeing luster.

"Ah!" thought the consumptive. "This peddler is a dreamer and a cynic. Perhaps he finds a peculiar significance in this profitless business of selling monkeys. He sees in his painted monkey the likeness of its higher analogue, man. To the peddler, perhaps, the monkey daubed with its thin coating of paint is man, smeared with the thin veneer of civilization. This mettlesome hopping and jumping, spinning and dancing of the monkey represents man, the puppet,

fuming turbulently under the strings held by king and war-lord, ex-
ploiter and slave-driver. Just as here and there on the monkey a gleam
of brightness reveals the metal, untouched by the paint; so too with
man, whose soul-devouring passions and prejudices, whose avarice
and blood-thirst reveal his baser self, untouched by the dissembling
veneer of civilization."

Suddenly the string snapped. The crazy gewgaw tottered defi-
antly a second, and then fell ungracefully to the snow-covered pavement.

"Aha! Aha! The monkey won't dance! He's broken his string!
That's what we've done—Elsie and I. We've broken the fettering
strings of society and are resolved to dance no longer!"

The consumptive moved on. He had promised Elsie that he
would return to her early. Near the end of the market block there
were booths where cedar trees and holly were sold. The wholesome
Christmas aroma came to him, and he stopped, searched through
several pockets, and having collected all of his change, bought the
largest holly wreath he saw. The purchase of the wreath was an unrea-
soned action; it simply completed a reflex caused by the stimulation
of the man's olfactory nerve centers by the cedars and holly.

Where the market ended, the street was narrow and dim-lit.
Ugly, old brick houses, the cellars of which quartered a heteroge-
neous array of tradesmen's mean shops, lined the street. In many of
the windows above the shops were lighted candles. Some windows,
uncurtained, revealed women and children decking Christmas trees.
After a time the man with the wreath turned into a street yet darker
and meaner and flanked with tall houses which made it seem more
narrow than it was. Here there were no shops, nor were there windows from which candles shone. The consumptive crept over the

crisp snow, and then he entered a house, passed through the black hallway, and groped his way up a flight of resounding, bare stairs. He paused at the first landing to recover his panting breath. He listened to his labored breathing as it rattled ominously in the frosty air; and there in the darkness, he smiled. Then, after climbing wearily the remaining three flights, he opened a door and entered a long room, which offered a sudden antithesis to anything the dismal appearance of the street would have presaged.

The room was well carpeted and was warmed by an open hearth. A reading lamp on a sturdy oaken table cast its glow over books and magazines lying there. In one corner, where the light but faintly reached, the blackness of a low piano blended with the shadows. The farther end of the room was screened off. The consumptive went behind the screens. There in an ancient, wooden bed beneath snowy covers a woman was sleeping lightly. The brilliancy of her abundant, black hair enhanced the white purity of its background. Her face, half-clouded by a capricious shadow, was composed and untroubled. Suddenly, as if informed by some strange telepathy of the watcher beside her bed, she awoke and gazed up into his haggard face.

"Jim," she said, "did the druggist let you have it?"

"Yes, Elsie. It was easy. How do you feel?"

"Rested now, Jim. What's that? Oh, holly! It's only a few hours before Christmas, isn't it? Do you know, Jim that I was born just thirty years ago tomorrow, on Christmas Day?"

"No, I didn't know it, dear. We've never talked birthdays, but I could have guessed that you were born on Christmas or Easter or on some Holy Day."

"Holy Day, Jim? No, Jim. There are no days holy in themselves; they're all alike unless people hallow them in their hearts and consciences. But most people don't hallow them inwardly. They use meaningless symbols like that holly wreath."

He hung the wreath on a post at the foot of the bed, and then took from his pocket two packages and placed them on a small table beside the bed. The woman saw the packages and her somber eyes sparkled.

"What's the larger package, Jim?"

"The bottle? Oh, that's champagne from Champagne, or as we had to call it when on furloughs from Hell, 'Du vin blanc.' " And he smiled weakly, and began feverishly to unbutton his overcoat.

But the eyes of woman are all-seeing; moreover, her intuition is mercurial and unerring.

"What's the trouble, Jim?"

"Nothing, dear. What makes you ask?"

"You're not as confident as when you went out. You seem excited."

"It's nothing. But, Elsie, I've been thinking about things, and about you. I've been wondering whether you have ever really cared that we weren't legally married."

"Oh, Jim! Why do you ask me that? No, I've never cared. I've never really thought about marriage. There were too many difficulties. Even if you had been well, our life would have been chiefly with ourselves. Marriage, too, would have been too sensational. The officials would have detected that I'm not white, and if they hadn't I couldn't lie about it. I would have told. And then, Jim, just imagine the newspaper stories and the editorials ranting of intermarriage and—"

"Don't, Elsie, don't! The fools who write newspapers don't know that in reality any marriage is an intermarriage. There must be some interchange, some blending, whether it be of dissimilar blood or of other qualities. I love you because you have every spiritual quality that I don't have, and because you are beautiful, because you are loyal, because your voice is gentle and soft, because your music charms me. You've been what any real mate is—a complement. As for the newspapers, had I been a well man, and had you wanted marriage, that would have come first, despite newspapers or anything else. As it was, I had no right to ask you to tie yourself to a weak and gloomy skeleton."

He stopped. Elsie was gazing steadfastly at him, and he continued:

"But this illness has changed my ideas; indeed—who knows—it may have clarified them, for now I hate the world that would deny me honest happiness after making me a weakling. God! How I detest men's pharisaic exactions and their smug conceits! I don't see how I could bring myself now to stoop to even one of their conventions.

"And, Elsie, you've been my comforter. You've listened to my ravings and quieted them. You've saved me from genuine misery and folly. And all this you've done for a wreck—a mere broken clod."

"Don't brood, Jim. You must not."

"I don't mean to, Elsie; but I've been thinking that it isn't fair to persuade you to do this—to go with me if you're not altogether willing."

"It's all settled now, Jim. I've been thinking too while you were away, and I now know that I don't want to do anything else—and I won't do anything else."

Reverently, Jim bent down and kissed her smooth forehead. Then, as if not completely assured, he said:

"If you're not sure, Elsie, I can go alone."

"Never mind, Jim: we're going together. I won't be separated from you. It's not your fault things haven't gone well. It's just been Fate."

Then, as if motivated by some slow passion welling up from the depths of his spirit, Jim again bent over the bed and kissed the woman, not quickly, or impulsively, but deliberately, first her forehead, then her cheeks and her lips.

He turned away and with head bowed walked beyond the screens. . . .

When he returned, he sat on the edge of the bed. The woman drew close and he enclosed her in his arm.

"Do you know, Jim, this has been a glorious experience—just two of us, living one for the other with nothing else to live for? I sometimes think that neither of us would have been happy if Fate had kept us apart. The sanction of the world for us, and for all like us, is only fair, but I doubt, Jim, if sanction could have made us any happier. . . . I wonder if the newspapers will get our story? Yes, I can see it now, headlines and all!"

"I don't mind that, Elsie. The thing that I don't like is that I don't know what will be done with us, going in this way."

"What's found won't be us, Jim, dear. But let's not worry these few minutes. Let's not even talk. Let's just think and be happy."

She nestled closer as if she thought that physical touch would foster that spiritual communion that she desired.

He was content. Whatever doubt he had as to the fairness of taking her with him was overcome by her earnest and tender devotion. She would have it no other way. She was his now and eternally. . . .

An hour passed, and bells, not sweet-toned from some rich temple, but harsh and mechanical began tolling the Christmas tide in.

"Are you ready, Jim?" she whispered.

"Yes, dear. Are you?"

"Yes," she murmured.

He reached to the table beside the bed for the smaller package. As he shook its contents into a glass, he smiled at the grinning death's-head the red label blazoned. There was a delightful tinkling sound as the champagne bottle in his weak and shaking hand kissed the rim of the glass into which the liquid gurgled.

He handed her the glass, and with his free arm drew her close to him.

She drank.

He took the glass, drank, and dropped it.

The bells rang on. . . .

They were drowsy now, but still conscious. Their embrace tightened.

The bells ceased.

UNCLE U.S. SANTA CLAUS

James Conway Jackson

In the early twentieth century, at the beginning of the Great
Migration, in 1913, James Conway Jackson wrote "Uncle U.S.
Santa Claus," a provocative narrative poem that challenges the
federal government to address the myriad of issues confronting
African Americans who were leaving the South in droves to escape
lynching, rank poverty, segregation, discrimination, and political
exclusion. Simply put, they were in search of a new freedom!
The poem is a powerful plea to the US government to honor the
Civil War amendments to the Constitution that granted African
Americans freedom and citizenship rights. What better time to raise
these questions than the early twentieth century, and what better
figure to employ as Santa Claus than good old "Uncle Sam," a
popular symbol of the US government.

✷ ✷ ✷ ✷ ✷

Uncle U.S. Santa Claus

While you're passing Christmas presents
    so promiscuously,
Please remember, Uncle U.S., that
    all people are not free;
Quite ten million faithful black folks
    are being treated quite unjust
It does seem, dear Uncle U.S., that
    you have betrayed our trust.

While the Christmas bells are ringing
    out so merrily,
Uncle Samuel, let that old bell ring
    again sweet liberty;
Let her ring in tones of thunder,
    North and South and East and West,
Until Right and Truth and Justice
    thrill the heart of every breast.

As your children, Uncle Samuel, we
    have rights you see;
Lincoln truly said this "nation cannot
    live half free;"
We demand that "Social Justice"
    others prate about,
And we humbly ask the reason why
    we were left out.

While the Christmas bells are ringing
　　out so long and loud,
Civil rights and social justice hide
　　behind a cloud;
Prejudice and Jim Crowism, vultures
　　from the South,
Seek to ROB the Government's Black
　　Folks' FOOD OUT of their mouth.

While the Christmas chimes are chiming
　　good will toward men,
We are ignored at the White House,
　　both by word and pen;
Peace and good will to all people
　　from the White House seems to mean
That the black folks of this country
　　are not counted in the scheme.

While the Christmas bells are ringing,
　　hear us, Lord, we pray!
Let the hearts of those that hate us
　　soften day by day;
Grant that e'er another Christmas
　　chimes forth merrily
That all nations and All People shall
　　be Wholly Free.

THE DEVIL SPENDS
CHRISTMAS EVE IN DIXIE
Andrew Dobson

Dr. Andrew Dobson was a well-known radio personality and journalist in Chicago during the 1930s. He appeared on local radio stations and nationally on NBC and CBS Radio. Referring to his abilities as an actor and as a comedian, Chicago newspaper editors called him "a Bert Williams . . . and Will Rogers of the Race all rolled into one." Dobson played the role of Old Uncle Joe on radio station WJJD, where he delighted his audience with songs and a rhyming philosophy that focused on topics of the time. In 1935, the *Chicago Defender* invited Dobson to write a weekly column called "Uncle Joe Dobson's Journal," a blend of African American folklore and old-fashioned philosophy applied to the issues of the day.

In "The Devil Spends Christmas Eve in Dixie," a poem published in 1934, Dobson uses the Christmas theme to bring attention to both the practice of lynching and to the Costigan-Wagner anti-lynching bill pending before the US Congress, one of several bills introduced in Congress between 1919 and 1935 as a response to the efforts of the NAACP to secure passage of a federal law outlawing the practice. Dobson was not alone in his commentary on lynching. Numerous writers, politicians, ministers, educators, musicians, and graphic artists used every opportunity to bring attention to the immoral and barbaric act. In 1939, Abel Meeropol, as Lewis Allan, wrote "Strange Fruit," a protest against lynching and racial violence. The song describes the bodies of lynching victims hanging from trees in the South and was popularized in the 1940s by jazz singer Billie Holiday. Like Dobson and other public figures, Holiday called attention to the brutal practice and demanded that the American government put an end to it. Dobson suggests that Christmas is heralded as a time for peace and good will to all men, however, "The Devil Spends Christmas Eve in Dixie."

The Devil Spends Christmas Eve in Dixie

Twas de night befo Christmas, where de devil holds sway
He ordered his imps to "knock off" fer de day
Says he: "Boys, bank yo fires. Put yo forks on de rack
We goin to America. We'll be late gittin back

As dey celebrates Christmas I wants you'll to see
I wants you to watch how dey decorates trees
You will heah Christmas Carols. You will see candles bright
Cause we goin to de place where dey celebrates right.

So put on yo wings. We'll fly South through de air
You won't need no coats cause dey's plenty hell dere.
Some imps spied de Statue of Liberty below
Dey started to wonder and fly kinda slow.

De devil looked back and sed: "Hey! flap dem wings"
"Nev mine dat statue cause it don't mean a thing."
Well dey all kept a flyin til one imp up and spoke.
He yells to de devil sayin: "Pa, what's dat smoke?"

De devil say: "Where?" Den he say: "Dats a cinch,"
"When dey's bonfires in Dixie dey's a black man to lynch."

Den de imps started pointing, cryin: "Look on dem trees,"
"Dey jus loaded with humans. Will you splain all dat please?"

Den old Satan started talkin and a wavin his hands
Says: "Chillun, its Christmas and you in Dixie land."
"Hate is so strong heah and love is so slack,
"Stead o lightin a candle dey sets fire to a black."

"Mos folks hang dey presents den go off to bed,
"Dey use Negroes in Dixie and dey hangs em till dead."
"Dey sings our kinda carols, songs of hate, greed and lust,
"Dey use mobs fer de choirs. Hear em now. My, what fuss."

"De bass in de choir is de baying of hounds,
"De blacks scream sopraner as de mobs run em down.
Den de imps tuk de air with a screech and a yell
Sayin: "We headin fer home. Dis America is hell."

"And dat," sed de devil as he howled with glee,
"Is de land of de brave and de home of de free."

ONE CHRISTMAS EVE
Langston Hughes

Langston Hughes was born in Joplin, Missouri, in 1902. His grandfather had been a radical abolitionist, his mother had a predilection for acting and writing poetry, and his father studied law. Gaining recognition in 1921 for writing "The Negro Speaks of Rivers," his most celebrated poem, Hughes became one of the most acclaimed of the poets, novelists, and dramatists of the twentieth century. He published at least eight volumes of poetry, including *The Weary Blues* (1926), *Fine Clothes to the Jew* (1927), *The Dream Keeper and Other Poems* (1932), *Shakespeare in Harlem* (1942), *Fields of Wonder* (1947), *One Way Ticket* (1949), *Montage of a Dream Deferred* (1951), *Ask Your Mama: 12 Moods for Jazz* (1961), and *The Panther and the Lash* (1967). His fiction was published in six novels—*Not Without Laughter* (1930), *Simple Speaks His Mind* (1950), *Simple Takes a Wife* (1953), *Simple Stakes a Claim* (1957), *Tambourines to Glory* (1958), and *Simple's Uncle Sam* (1965)—and in three volumes of short stories: *The Ways of White Folks* (1934), *Laughing to Keep from Crying* (1952), and *Something in Common and Other Stories* (1963).

"One Christmas Eve" was published in *Opportunity* in December 1933. The editor noted, "Langston Hughes, just returned from a lengthy stay in Russia, turns his hand to the short story and shows a growing mastery of that medium." Prior to going to the Soviet Union in 1932, Hughes, at the insistence of the noted educator Mary McLeod Bethune, travelled throughout the South reading to mainly black audiences. Listening to the stories of black Southerners, and personally experiencing segregation and discrimination at every turn, Hughes became inspired to write this story.

In 1930, the majority of African American women were employed as domestics. In many small Southern towns, such as the one described here by Hughes, educated and uneducated African American women and men had few economic opportunities. As late as 1990, the majority of black women, many without formal education, were employed mostly in service positions and agriculture. Teaching and preaching were the primary professional employments open to educated blacks. Arcie, the central character of this story, personifies the plight of some black servants and of many African American women who worked to support their families as domestics. A single woman with a young child, Arcie works long hours for meager wages, which barely support her basic needs. Yet, with all her problems, she yearns to provide her child with a "normal" Christmas.

Hughes demonstrates Arcie's efforts to make Christmas a happy occasion for Joe, her four-year-old son, and employs the Christmas theme to illustrate the vast economic gap between whites and blacks, and the lack of concern evidenced by some whites about the lives of their servants. As John Henrik Clarke does in the story "Santa Claus Is a White Man," Hughes examines the meaning of Santa Claus for black children, especially boys.

Hughes's Santa Claus, like Clarke's, does not see Joe simply as a child who, like all children, idolizes Santa and believes in his goodness. For Santa Claus, Joe is just a Negro, a reviled figure to be made fun of, an animal without humanity, and a beast of burden to be used. Like all children who gravitate toward Santa Claus, Joe sees no reason why he should not enter the lobby of a segregated movie theatre where Santa is dispensing gifts and good cheer.

Because of the particular vulnerability of black males to lynching and other racial attacks, Hughes and Clarke used black boys to demonstrate the problem black parents faced in trying to provide a "normal" childhood for their children, while at the same time educating them about what it meant to be black in America. The dilemma that African American parents, particularly Southern blacks, confronted each December was how to celebrate and embrace America's definition of Christmas and Santa Claus, and at the same time protect their children from the dangers posed by racism, inherent in every aspect of United States culture—even Christmas.

One Christmas Eve

Standing over the hot stove cooking supper, the colored maid, Arcie, was very tired. Between meals today, she had cleaned the whole house for the white family she worked for, getting ready for Christmas tomorrow. Now her back ached and her head felt faint from sheer fatigue. Well, she would be off in a little while, if only the Missus and her children would come on home to dinner. They were out shopping for more things for the tree which stood all ready, tinsel-hung and lovely in the living room, waiting for its candles to be lighted.

Arcie wished she could afford a tree for Joe. He'd never had one yet, and it's nice to have such things when you're little. Joe was five, going on six. Arcie, looking at the roast in the white folks' oven, wondered how much she could afford to spend tonight on toys for Joe. She only got seven dollars a week, and four of that went for her room and the landlady's daily looking after Joe while Arcie was at work.

"Lord, it's more'n a notion raisin' a child," she thought.

She looked at the clock on the kitchen table. After seven. What made white folks so inconsiderate, she wondered. Why didn't they come on home here to supper? They knew she wanted to get off before all the stores closed. She wouldn't have time to buy Joe nothin' if they didn't hurry. And her landlady probably wanting to go out and shop, too, and not be bothered with little Joe.

"Doggone it!" Arcie said to herself. "If I just had my money, I might leave the supper on the stove for 'em. I just got to get to the stores fo' they close." But she hadn't been paid for the week yet. The Missus had promised to pay her Christmas Eve, a day or so ahead of time.

Arcie heard a door slam and talking and laughter in the front of the house. She went in and saw the Missus and her kids shaking snow off their coats.

"Umm-m! It's swell for Christmas Eve," one of the kids said to Arcie. "It's snowin' like the deuce, and mother came near driving through a stop light. Can't hardly see for the snow. It's swell!"

"Supper's ready," Arcie said. She was thinking how her shoes weren't very good for walking in snow.

It seemed like the white folks took as long as they could to eat that evening. While Arcie was washing dishes, the Missus came out with her money.

"Arcie," the Missus said, "I'm so sorry, but would you mind if I just gave you five dollars tonight? The children have made me run short of change, buying presents and all."

"I'd like to have seven," Arcie said. "I needs it."

"Well, I just haven't got seven," the Missus said. "I didn't know you'd want all your money before the end of the week, anyhow. I just haven't got it to spare."

Arcie took five. Coming out of the hot kitchen, she wrapped up as well as she could and hurried by the house where she roomed to get little Joe. At least he could look at the Christmas trees in the windows downtown.

The landlady, a big light yellow woman, was in a bad humor. She said to Arcie, "I thought you was comin' home early and get this child. I guess you know I want to go out, too, once in a while."

Arcie didn't say anything, for if she had, she knew the landlady would probably throw it up to her that she wasn't getting paid to look after a child both night and day.

"Come on, Joe," Arcie said to her son, "Let's us go in the street."

"I hears they got a Santa Claus down town," Joe said, wriggling into his worn little coat. "I want to see him."

"Don't know 'bout that," his mother said, "But hurry up and get your rubbers on. Stores'll be closed directly."

It was six or eight blocks downtown. They trudged along

through the falling snow, both of them a little cold. But the snow was pretty!

The main street was hung with bright red and blue lights. In front of the City Hall there was a Christmas tree—but it didn't have no presents on it, only lights. In the store windows there were lots of toys—for sale.

Joe kept on saying, "Mama, I want. . . ."

But mama kept walking ahead. It was nearly ten, when the stores were due to close, and Arcie wanted to get Joe some cheap gloves and something to keep him warm, as well as a toy or two. She thought she might come across a rummage sale where they had children's clothes. And in the ten-cent store, she could get some toys.

"O-oo! Lookee. . . . ," little Joe kept saying, and pointing at things in the windows. How warm and pretty the lights were, and the shops, and the electric signs through the snow.

It took Arcie more than a dollar to get Joe's mittens and things he needed. In the A&P Arcie bought a big box of hard candies for 49 cents. And then she guided Joe through the crowd on the street until they came to the dime store. Near the ten-cent store they passed a moving picture theatre. Joe said he wanted to go in and see the movies.

Arcie said, "Ump un! No, child. This ain't Baltimore where they have shows for colored, too. In these here small towns, they don't let colored folks in. We can't go in there."

"Oh," said little Joe.

In the ten-cent store, there was an awful crowd. Arcie told Joe to stand outside and wait for her. Keeping hold of him in the crowded store would be a job. Besides she didn't want him to see what toys she was buying. They were to be a surprise from Santa Claus tomorrow.

Little Joe stood outside the ten-cent store in the light, and the snow, and people passing. Gee, Christmas was pretty. All tinsel and stars and cotton. And Santa Claus a-coming from somewhere, dropping things in stockings. And all the people in the streets were carrying things, and the kids looked happy.

But Joe soon got tired of just standing and thinking and waiting in front of the ten-cent store. There were so many things to look at in the other windows. He moved along up the block a little, and then a little more, walking and looking. In fact, he moved until he came to the picture show.

In the lobby of the moving picture show, behind the plate glass doors, it was all warm and glowing and awful pretty. Joe stood looking in, and as he looked his eyes began to make out, in there blazing beneath holly and colored streamers and the electric stars of the lobby, a marvelous Christmas tree. A group of children and grown-ups, white, of course, were standing around a big man in red beside the tree. Or was it a man? Little Joe's eyes opened wide. No, it was not a man at all. It was Santa Claus!

Little Joe pushed open one of the glass doors and ran into the lobby of the white moving picture show. Little Joe went right through the crowd and up to where he could get a good look at Santa Claus. And Santa Claus was giving away gifts, little presents for children, little boxes of animal crackers and stick-candy canes. And behind him on the tree was a big sign, (which little Joe didn't know how to read). It said, to those who understood, Merry Christmas from Santa Claus to our young patrons. Around the lobby, other signs said, When you come out of the show stop with your children and see our Santa Claus. And another announced, Gem Theatre makes its customers happy—see our Santa.

And there was Santa Claus in a red suit and a white beard all sprinkled with tinsel snow. Around him were rattles and drums and rocking horses which he was not giving away. But the signs on them said (could little Joe have read) that they would be presented from the stage on Christmas Day to the holders of lucky numbers. Tonight, Santa Claus was only giving away candy, and stick-candy canes, and animal crackers to the kids.

Joe would have liked terribly to have a stick-candy cane. He came a little closer to Santa Claus. He was right in the front of the crowd. And then Santa Claus saw Joe.

Why is it that lots of white people always grin when they see a Negro child? Santa Claus grinned. Everybody else grinned, too, looking at little black Joe—who had no business in the lobby of a white theatre. Then Santa Claus stooped down and slyly picked up one of his lucky number rattles, a great big loud tin-pan rattle like they use in cabarets. And he shook it fiercely right at Joe. That was funny. The white people laughed, kids and all. But little Joe didn't laugh. He was scared. To the shaking of the big rattle, he turned and fled out of the warm lobby of the theatre, out into the street where the snow was and the people. Frightened by laughter, he had begun to cry. He went looking for his mama. In his heart he never thought Santa Claus shook great rattles at children like that—and then laughed.

In the crowd on the street he went the wrong way. He couldn't find the ten-cent store or his mother. There were too many people, all white people, moving like white shadows in the snow, a world of white people.

It seemed to Joe an awfully long time till he suddenly saw Arcie, dark and worried-looking, cut across the side-walk through the passing crowd and grab him. Although her arms were full of packages, she still managed with one free hand to shake him until his teeth rattled.

"Why didn't you stand there where I left you?" Arcie demanded loudly. "Tired as I am, I got to run all over the streets in the night lookin' for you. I'm a great mind to wear you out."

When little Joe got his breath back, on the way home, he told his mama he had been in the moving picture show.

"But Santa Claus didn't give me nothin'," Joe said tearfully. "He made a big noise at me and I runned out."

"Serves you right," said Arcie, trudging through the snow. "You had no business in there. I told you to stay where I left you."

"But I seed Santa Claus in there," little Joe said, "so I went in."

"Huh! That wasn't no Santa Claus," Arcie explained. "If it was, he wouldn't a-treated you like that. That's a theatre for white folks— I told you once—and he's just a old white man."

"Oh. . . . ," said little Joe.

SANTA CLAUS
IS A WHITE MAN
John Henrik Clarke

John Henrik Clarke, a sharecropper's son, was born in Alabama
in 1915 but grew up in Columbus, Georgia. In 1933, attracted
by tales of the literary and cultural developments spawned by the
Harlem Renaissance, he traveled to New York to study creative
writing at Columbia University. Immersing himself in the creative
and political activities that flourished in Harlem, he was publishing
his short stories, poems, articles, and book reviews in magazines
and newspapers within a short span of years. During the early
years of his career, Clarke was the cofounder and fiction editor
of the *Harlem Quarterly*, the book review editor of the *Negro
History Bulletin*, an associate editor of *Freedomways* magazine,
and a contributor and feature writer for several African and
African American newspapers. Clarke wrote six books, edited and
contributed to seventeen others, composed more than fifty short
stories, published articles and pamphlets, and helped to found or
edit several important black periodicals. His edited collections
included *American Negro Short Stories* (1966), *Malcolm X: The Man
and His Times* (1969), *Harlem U.S.A.* (1971), and *Marcus Garvey
and the Vision of Africa* (1973).

At his death, in July 1998, Clarke was described in the *New York Times'* obituary as "an academic original." This tribute paid homage to a man who was in essence an American original. Historically, he is among the few people who were able to obtain an academic teaching position at a major institution of learning without benefit of formal training. Beginning as a lecturer in 1969, Clarke enjoyed a long and distinguished tenure as a professor of black and Puerto Rican Studies at Hunter College in New York City and established the Black Studies program there. A largely self-educated man, Clarke was an eighth-grade dropout who eventually took courses at New York University and Columbia. He earned a doctorate in 1993. Through his teachings, writings, and speeches, he distinguished himself as one of the leading black intellectuals of his time. Known as a scholar of African history, he spurred the movement to develop the field of black studies and became one of Harlem's leading intellectuals.

"Santa Claus Is a White Man" explores the multidimensionality of Southern racism and explodes the myth about the goodness of Santa Claus. As a cultural icon, Santa Claus enjoyed a mythical status, which defined him as a benevolent figure whose legendary love and generosity transcended the boundaries of race, religion, class, and ethnicity. However, the Southern white Santa Claus could, in fact, be the opposite of this image and could pose a threat to a black person's very existence.

Focusing on the central character, Randolph Johnson, "the happiest little colored boy in all Louisiana," Clarke demonstrates the need for black parents to educate their children about the real identity of Santa Claus and uses social realism to tell the story of how little value a black life had during the era of lynching in the South.

Santa Claus Is a White Man

When he left the large house where his mother was a servant, he was happy. She had embraced him lovingly and had given him—for the first time in his life!—a quarter. "Now you go do your Chris'mus shopping," she had said. "Get somethin' for Daddy and something for Baby and something for Aunt Lil. And something for Mummy too, if it's any money left."

He had already decided how he would divide his fortune. A nickel for something for Daddy, another nickel for Baby, another for Aunt Lil. And ten whole cents for Mummy's present. Something beautiful and gorgeous, like a string of pearls, out of the ten-cent store.

His stubby legs moved fast as he headed toward the business district. Although it was mid-December, the warm southern sun brought perspiration flooding to his little, dark skinned face. He was so happy . . . exceedingly happy! Effortlessly he moved along, feeling light and free, as if the wind was going to swoop him up to the heavens, up where everybody could see him—Randolph Johnson, the happiest little colored boy in all Louisiana!

When he reached the outskirts of the business district, where the bulk of the city's poor-whites lived, he slowed his pace. He felt instinctively that if he ran, one of them would accuse him of having stolen something; and if he moved too slow, he might be charged with looking for something to steal. He walked along with quick, cautious strides, glancing about fearfully now and then. Temporarily the happiness which the prospect of going Christmas shopping had brought him was subdued.

He passed a bedraggled Santa Claus, waving a tinny bell beside a cardboard chimney. He did not hesitate even when the tall fat man smiled at him through whiskers that were obviously cotton. He had seen the one real Santa weeks ago, in a big department store downtown, and had asked for all the things he wanted. This forlorn figure was merely one of Santa's helpers, and he had no time to waste on him just at the moment.

Further down the street he could see a gang of white boys, urchins of the street, clustered about an outdoor fruit stand. They were stealing apples, he was sure. He saw the white-aproned proprietor rush out; saw them disperse in all directions like a startled flock of birds, then gather together again only a few hundred feet ahead of him.

Apprehension surged through his body as the eyes of the gang leader fell upon him. Fear gripped his heart, and his brisk pace slowed to a cautious walk. He decided to cross the street to avoid the possibility of an encounter with this group of dirty ragged white boys.

As he stepped from the curb the voice of the gang leader barked a sharp command. "Hey you, come here!"

The strange, uncomfortable fear within him grew. His eyes widened and every muscle in his body trembled with sudden uneasiness. He started to run, but before he could do so a wall of human flesh had been pushed around him. He was forced back onto the sidewalk, and each time he tried to slip through the crowd of laughing white boys he was shoved back abruptly by the red-headed youngster who led the others.

He gazed dumbfoundedly over the milling throng which was surrounding him, and was surprised to see that older persons, passersby, had joined to watch the fun. He looked back up the street, hopefully, toward the bell-ringing Santa Claus, and was surprised to find him calmly looking on from a safe distance, apparently enjoying the excitement.

He could see now that there was no chance to escape the gang until they let him go, so he just stood struggling desperately to steady his trembling form. His lips twitched nervously and the perspiration on his round black face reflected a dull glow. He could not think; his mind was heavy with confusion.

The red-headed boy was evidently the leader. He possessed a robustness that set him off from the others. They stared impatiently at him, waiting for his next move. He shifted his position awkwardly and spoke with all the scorn that he could muster:

"Whereya goin', nigger? An' don't you know we don't allow niggers in this neighborhood?"

His tone wasn't as harsh as he had meant it to be. It sounded a bit like poor play-acting.

"I'm jes' goin' to the ten-cent store," the little black boy said meekly. "Do my Chris'mus shopping."

He scanned the crowd hurriedly, hoping there might be a chance of escape. But he was completely engulfed. The wall of people about him was rapidly thickening; restless, curious people, laughing at him because he was frightened. Laughing and sneering at a little colored boy who had done nothing wrong, and harmed no one.

He began to cry. "Please, lemme go. I ain't done nothin'."

One of the boys said, "Aw, let 'im go." His suggestion was

abruptly laughed down. The red-headed boy held up his hand. "Wait a minute, fellers," he said. "This nigger's goin' shoppin', he must have money, huh? Maybe we oughta see how much he's got."

The little black boy pushed his hand deeper into his pocket and clutched his quarter frantically. He looked about the outskirts of the crowd for a sympathetic adult face. He saw only the fat, sloppy-looking white man in the bedraggled Santa Claus suit that he had passed a moment earlier. This strange, cotton-bearded apparition was shoving his way now through the cluster of people, shifting his huge body along in gawky, poorly timed strides like a person cursed with a subnormal mentality.

When he reached the center of the circle within which the frightened boy was trapped, he waved the red-haired youth aside and, yanking off his flowing whiskers, took command of the situation.

"What's yo' name, niggah?" he demanded.

The colored boy swallowed hard. He was more stunned than frightened; never in his life had he imagined Santa—or even one of Santa's helpers—in a role like this.

"My name's Randolph," he got out finally.

A smile wrinkled the leathery face of the man in the tattered red suit.

"Randolph," he exclaimed, and there was a note of mockery in his tone. "Dat's no name fer er niggah! No Niggah's got no business wit er nice name like dat!" Then, bringing his broad hand down forcefully on the boy's shoulder, he added, "Heah after yo' name's Jem!"

His words boomed over the crowd in a loud, brusque tone, defying all other sound. A series of submerged giggles sprang up among the boys as they crowded closer to get a better glimpse of the unmasked Santa Claus and the little colored boy.

The latter seemed to have been decreasing in size under the heavy intensity of their gaze. Tears mingled with the perspiration flooding his round black face. Numbness gripped his body.

"Kin I go on now?" he pleaded. His pitifully weak tone was barely audible. "My momma told me to go straight to the ten-cent store. I ain't been botherin' nobody."

"If you don't stop dat damn cryin,' we'll send you t'see Saint Peter." The fat white man spoke with anger and disgust. The cords in his neck quivered and new color came to his rough face, lessening its haggardness. He paused as if reconsidering what he had just said, then added: "Second thought, don't think we will . . . Don't think Saint Peter would have anything t' do with a nigger."

The boys laughed long and heartily. When their laughter diminished, the red-coated man shifted his gawky figure closer to the little Negro and scanned the crowd, impatient and undecided.

"Let's lynch 'im," one of the youths cried.

"Yeah, let's lynch 'im!" another shouted, much louder and with more enthusiasm.

As if these words had some magic attached to them, they swept through the crowd. Laughter, sneers, and queer, indistinguishable mutterings mingled together.

Anguish was written on the boy's dark face.

Desperately he looked about for a sympathetic countenance.

The words, "Let's lynch him," were a song now, and the song was floating through the December air, mingling with the sounds of tangled traffic.

"I'll get a rope!" the red-haired boy exclaimed. Wedging his way through the crowd, he shouted gleefully, "Just wait'll I get back!"

Gradually an ominous hush fell over the crowd. They stared questioningly, first at the frightened boy, then at the fat man dressed like Santa Claus who towered over him.

"What's that you got in yo' pocket?" the fat man demanded suddenly.

Frightened, the boy quickly withdrew his hands from his pockets and put them behind his back. The white man seized the right one and forced it open. On seeing its contents, his eyes glittered with delight.

"Ah, a quarter!" he exclaimed. "Now tell me, niggah, where in th' hell did you steal this?"

"Didn't steal hit," the boy tried to explain. "My momma gived it to me."

"Momma gived it to you, heh?" The erstwhile Santa Claus snorted. He took the quarter and put it in a pocket of his red suit. "Niggahs ain't got no business wit' money whilst white folks is starving," he said. "I'll jes keep this quarter for myself."

Worry spread deep lines across the black boy's forehead. His lips parted, letting out a short, muted sob. The crowd around him seemed to blur.

As far as his eyes could see, there were only white people all about him. One and all they sided with the curiously out-of-place Santa Claus. Ill-nourished children, their dirty, freckled faces lighted up in laughter. Men clad in dirty overalls, showing their tobacco-stained teeth. Women, whose rutted faces had never known cosmetics, moved their bodies restlessly in their soiled housedresses.

Here suddenly the red-coated figure held up his hand for silence. He looked down at the little black boy and a new expression was on his face. It was not pity; it was more akin to a deep irksomeness. When the crowd quieted slightly, he spoke.

"Folks," he began hesitantly, "ah think this niggah's too lil'l t' lynch. Besides, it's Christmas time . . ."

"Well," a fat man answered slowly, "it jus' ain't late 'nuf in the season. 'Taint got cold yet round these parts. In this weather a lynched niggah would make the whole neighborhood smell bad."

A series of disappointed grunts belched up from the crowd. Some laughed; others stared protestingly at the red-coated white man. They were hardly pleased with his decision.

However, when the red-haired boy returned with a length of rope, the "let's lynch 'im" song had died down. He handed the rope to the white man, who took it and turned it over slowly in his gnarled hands.

"Sorry, sonny," he said. His tone was dry, with a slight tremor. He was not firmly convinced that the decision he had reached was the best one. "We sided not to lynch him; he's too lil'l and it's too warm yet. And besides, what's one lil'l niggah who ain't ripe enough to be lynched? Let's let 'im live awhile . . . maybe we'll get 'im later."

The boy frowned angrily. "Aw, you guys!" he groaned. "T' think of all th' trouble I went to gettin' that rope . . ."

In a swift, frenzied gesture his hand was raised to strike the little black boy, who curled up, more terrified than ever. But the bedraggled Santa stepped between them.

"Wait a minute, sonny," he said. "Look a here." He put his

hand in the pocket of his suit and brought forth the quarter, which he handed to the red-haired boy.

A smile came to the white youth's face and flourished into jubilant laughter. He turned the quarter from one side to the other in the palm of his hand, marveling at it. Then he held it up so the crowd could see it, and shouted gleefully, "Sure there's a Santa Claus!"

The crowd laughed heartily.

Still engulfed by the huge throng, still bewildered beyond words, the crestfallen little colored boy stood whimpering. They had taken his fortune from him and there was nothing he could do about it. He didn't know what to think about Santa Claus now. About anything, in fact.

He saw that the crowd was falling back, that in a moment there would be a path through which he could run. He waited until it opened, then sped through it as fast as his stubby legs could carry him. With every step a feeling of thankfulness swelled within him.

The red-haired boy who had started the spectacle threw a rock after him. It fell short. The other boys shouted jovially, "Run, nigger, run!" The erstwhile Santa Claus began to read just his mask. The mingled chorus of jeers and laughter was behind the little colored boy pushing him on like a great invisible force. Most of the crowd stood on the side walk watching him until his form became vague and finally disappeared around a corner . . .

After a while he felt his legs weakening. He slowed down to a brisk walk, and soon found himself on the street that pointed toward his home.

Crestfallen, he looked down at his empty hands and thought of the shiny quarter that his mother had given him. He closed his right hand tightly, trying to pretend that it was still there. But that only hurt the more.

Gradually the fear and worry disappeared from his face. He was now among his neighbors, people that he knew. He felt bold and relieved. People smiled at him, said "Hello." The sun had dried his tears.

He decided he would tell no one, except his mother, of his ordeal. She, perhaps, would understand, and either give him a new quarter or do his shopping for him. But what would she say about that awful figure of a Santa Claus? He decided not to ask her. There were some things no one, not even mothers, could explain.

MERRY CHRISTMAS EVE
Adele Hamlin

A resident of Washington, DC, Adele Hamlin attended
Armstrong High School where she established a reputation as an
actor in the dramas put on by the school's dramatic club. In 1932,
the *Baltimore Afro American* described her performance of "Emma,
the maid" as "a scream." Her love of the theater fueled her interest
in writing plays that focused on black women's relationships with
men. And in short stories such as "Molly Ann: The Love Story
of an Unmarried Mother" and "A Rotten Filthy Coward," Hamlin
describes the lives of ordinary women who often fall in love and
sometime get pregnant by men who are simply interested in having
a good time. Hamlin's female characters are strong and outspoken
women who refuse to be humbled by these experiences.

Between 1931 and 1953, Adele Hamlin wrote more than
twenty short stories, including "The Christ Child Comes to
Town," "The Christmas Fair," and "A Bride for Christmas,"
all of which appeared in the *Baltimore Afro-American*. "Merry
Christmas Eve," published in 1948, is set on Christmas Eve
instead of the usual Christmas Day. The story revolves around
Angie, a young woman who is excited over her new relationship
with Doug, who is the exact opposite of her old boyfriend, Rollins.
Christmas Eve is considered by many to be a special time, to be

spent with those whom we love. For some, it is a time to evaluate old relationships and to solidify new ones. In any case, it is conceived of as a time to be spent with those who make us feel good about life and ourselves.

Angie, like many young women, finds it difficult to move forward with a new relationship without coming to closure with the old. To do so, she uses those values associated with Christmas to make careful comparisons between Doug and Rollins. The central question for Angie is, Which of them reflects the strength and character she is looking for in a man? For her, a virtuous man is one who is caring, unselfish, generous, responsible, and sensitive. That is the kind of man she wants to spend Christmas Eve, Christmas Day, and indeed the rest of her life with. Will Angie choose Doug or Rollins?

Merry Christmas Eve

The sun was up playing against the blinds. Angie sat up and laughed because it was Christmas Eve and Doug was coming over early that morning. Christmas was a glorious time to be with Doug, he was so gay, crazy, good and everything that took her mind off Rollins.

Jane had the radio on and children were singing "Santa Claus Is Coming to Town." Angie jumped up and joined them.

"It's bad luck to sing before breakfast!"

"I'm not superstitious on Christmas Eve!" she yelled down to her sister.

Dressed, she hurried downstairs. Wrapped gifts were on chairs and tables and a tree stood in a corner waiting to be dressed. She and Doug would do that before they went to church. A New Man!

"My," said Jane, "new hair-do, new clothes, new personality. Oh what a new man and be-bop glasses can do for a chick!"

"Any coffee?"

"Uh-huh. Not changing the subject but you look much better than you did when Rollins was around. Don't you feel better too? He was so darn morbid!"

"Leave Rollins out! I want to have a marvelous time this year!"

"Making up for the years Rollins spoiled. Or does Doug automatically make everything nice?"

"Doug and I are just good friends!" said Angie indignantly. "He's helping me forget Rollins and I'm helping him forget Alice!"

A Grand Job

"Well let me be the first to congratulate you two on the grand job you're doing!"

"Now look—Oh! There's Doug!"

"Imagine Rollins taking baskets to needy families. You might love Rollins but I bet you have more fun with Doug."

Doug held an armful of holly. "I saw a kid selling this—"

"And you bought the whole bunch!"

"I told him I wanted to decorate a hall."

Doug could help a person without taking away his self-respect.

During the deliveries he became bosom friends with the families. He repaired a tree holder, sang carols drank a glass of port with an old lady and played a few numbers with an old gentleman who couldn't find a job.

They crept through streets lined with people, Santa Clauses, Salvation Army kettles, Christmas trees, their salesmen huddled around cans of fire.

Jane met them at the door and blurted out, "Rollins called. He'll be over at eight."

Angie stared at her. "Rollins called?" she said wonderingly. She walked slowly to the window. She didn't know what to do or think. It was as if Christmas were over.

Doug spoke casually, "I guess I'll run along." He left before Angie could speak.

"Well your old flame is back," said Jane dryly. "Are you glad?"

"I don't know," said Angie. "I don't know." But all of a sudden she felt very tired.

The Same Rollins

Rollins came. The same old Rollins. His new suit cost him a hundred bucks so he hadn't minded tossing a quarter to a beggar as he hopped in a cab to come to her house.

Angie turned the radio on. She was thinking about Doug.

"Aren't you going to kiss me?"

"Later," she said avoiding his eyes.

His voice fell on her and seemed to smother her. She chinked at the smoldering logs. Sparks rushed up the chimney, the flames following.

"Weren't you wrong, Angie?"

As she gazed into the flames, she saw Doug's face.

"You could have called me and told me you were sorry."

She turned away from the fireplace but there was the radio. A choir was singing "Silent Night" and she could hear Doug with them.

"It doesn't take anything away from you to apologize—"

"Rollins, go away!" she cried.

After he left she stared into the fire until Jane and Harry were ready for church. She shook her head when they asked her to go with them.

She finally aroused herself and looked out the door at the quiet sky. It was a dark blue velvet with hundreds of stars.

"And once there was a star, brighter than all the rest, that led them from afar to The Holy Child—" She came back in and started dressing the tree.

And after a while the door chimes sounded gently. She stared about her.

The tree's fragrance began to fill the room, a sweet tenor voice began singing, "Oh Holy Night," and sparks from the fire began to dance merrily up the chimney—she rushed to the door.

"Doug!" she cried. "Oh Doug!"

She was in his arms and he was saying, "Baby, we're about to break up a beautiful friendship." He kissed her and said, "Merry Christmas, darling," and then he kissed her again.

WHITE CHRISTMAS
Valena Minor Williams

Valena Minor Williams enjoyed a long and distinguished career as
a journalist. Born in New Orleans in 1923, she received a bachelor
of science degree from Bennett College and a master's degree in
journalism from the University of California, Berkeley. During her
long and distinguished career, she served as a public broadcaster at
several radio stations in Cleveland and as a station manager in San
Francisco, as well as the producer and coordinator for university
relations in the President General's Office at UC Berkeley. She
was a professional member of the board of directors for National
Public Radio. Cited in *American Women in Radio and Television*,
Williams received the Golden Mike Award in 1962 for her series
of articles on race relations in Cleveland.

Williams wrote and published "White Christmas" in 1953, on
the eve of the modern civil rights movement. This story captures
the mood and attitudes of African Americans at a critical juncture
in US history. World War II had created a climate that made
it possible for blacks to make significant economic, social, and
political gains. As a result of continued migration to Northern and
Midwestern industrial centers, African Americans increased their
political power. Though legalized segregation and discrimination
prevailed throughout the South, and blacks in the North and West

were often the targets of discrimination in housing and employment, they no longer accepted their second-class citizenship as inevitable. There was an air of freedom in America, a feeling that change was coming. Throughout the world, people of color were gaining their freedom as colonialism came to an end in many countries. The impact of those events, and of the United Nations' support for the human rights of all people, signaled a change in attitude that was evident in the higher branches of the US government.

In the 1950s, many young people were aware of America's history of slavery and of the role blacks played in achieving their freedom. Those who gave their lives in the struggle were declared heroes; others were viewed as Uncle Toms. Resistance against white oppression, whether by word or deed, was viewed as an important part of the black struggle. Challenging the symbols of racism was a sign of courage, especially when it could mean the end of one's life or livelihood. In "White Christmas," Uncle Charlie understands the protocol of race and racism, for he has managed to walk that line and keep his "good" job at the exclusive country club where he works as the maître d'hôtel. Given the exceedingly limited employment opportunities available to black men during this time, this was considered an excellent job for someone with an education, let alone an uneducated person.

While Uncle Charlie and his sister, Ophelia, a "day worker" or domestic, accept the reality of their existence, John Thomas did not. Ophelia's ten-year-old son, John, lives with his Uncle Charlie in an impoverished neighborhood where he learns what it means to be a "colored" boy. He, like his counterparts, is critical of his elders and others whom he believes ingratiate themselves to whites and accept ill treatment. John respects and looks up to Uncle Charlie, whom he expects to be a "man" and challenge white racism. Uncle Charlie is keenly aware of the enormous responsibility he has for seeing that John understands who he is and that he develops confidence and a belief in himself.

In "White Christmas," Uncle Charlie gave his nephew John an indispensable Christmas gift, one that cannot be bought—he gave him back his self-respect!

White Christmas

It was beginning to snow, but young John Thomas didn't even seem to notice.

Uncle Charlie was worried about his ten-year-old nephew. Ten was a hard age for a boy even if he had a Daddy and even if he wasn't colored.

Uncle Charlie had watched John Thomas grow more and more quiet and he knew what that meant. It meant that the boy's world was constantly falling into two categories, the right or the wrong, the good or the bad, and, most important to young John Thomas these days, the white or the colored.

Ten is the age when most youngsters are taught there is something wrong with being colored.

"Look at that silly old Santa Claus," John Thomas sneered. "Pasty faced old goat. I hope he freezes."

The two passed the street-corner Santa but the boy's attack continued, "I'm sick of white Santa Clauses. Ain't there no colored ones, nowhere?" The boy didn't expect an answer to his question.

A Hard Struggle

Charlie thought about his sister, Ophelia. She had done the best she could with the boy since her husband had died.

She'd done day's work so that the youngsters would always have a clean place to live, enough to eat and clothes to wear. But she hadn't taken much time out to explain things to him.

She hadn't been able to cancel out the hard words that John Thomas was learning in school, the epithets, the talk of slums, disease, dirt and poverty that he was beginning to think were all a part of being colored.

Ophelia accepted her lot. Charlie could see John Thomas did not. He had seen the hurt in the sensitive child's face when once Ophelia had sighed wearily after a hard day's work, "It's a white man's world all right. Nothin' for no one else."

That's one reason Charlie had, year after year, taken John Thomas to the Christmas parties given at the exclusive country club where he worked. He wanted the boy to see beautiful surroundings.

Charlie had been maître d'hôtel for nearly twenty-five years and no one minded his bringing his big-eyed little nephew for the holiday festivities. And Charlie had plans for the boy's future.

Did Not Want to Go

There was always a towering, brightly-lighted tree, a Santa whom everyone knew was the Chef, and lots and lots of presents for everyone.

The first year John Thomas went, his eyes had lit up and he'd loved every moment of the brief wonder-world. Now he didn't want to go with his Uncle Charlie anymore.

Uncle Charlie couldn't be expected to understand how he felt. This club was his world.

Maybe his name should have been Uncle Tom instead of Uncle Charlie.

"That's all he is with his bowing and scraping to those big white folks," the boy thought savagely.

John Thomas didn't want any of that charity handed out to him.

He came in through the kitchen, so he didn't really belong at any party with millionaires' brats.

Too Much Spirit

The kids were nice enough, he admitted to himself grudgingly. It was the club members who stopped in to look at their children after a quick trip to the bar.

They were the ones who rubbed his head "for luck," or called him "Sunshine" or "Snowball."

Last year one flipped him a quarter "to buy himself a Cadillac." They were just full of "too much Christmas spirits," Uncle Charlie had explained. But it hurt anyhow.

"Here we are," John Thomas's Uncle Charlie's voice broke through the boy's dark thoughts. They were at the side door of the club.

"We're not going in through the kitchen?"

"No, we can go in the side. You go on and play with the children. You know most of the ones your age. I'll be in after I see how things are going."

"I'll go with you Uncle Charlie," the boy said, quietly, just to let his uncle know he knew where he really belonged.

The Chef's Sick

Uncle Charlie shrugged wearily. After hanging up their coats, they went into the warm high-ceilinged kitchen.

The long serving tables were cleared of all other food except trays of sandwiches and cookies and there was a steaming kettle of cocoa on the huge range. Party fare for the youngsters. But no one was there except Mr. Jenkins, the club president. He looked terribly upset.

"The children are all out there singing and waiting for Santa Claus to appear, Charlie. And Chef's gone home sick. Who in the world can we get to play Santa Claus?"

Mr. Jenkins held the bright red Santa suit in his hand and kept peeping through the tiny windows in the kitchen door as if he could actually see the children in the Assembly Room.

"Chef sick?" Uncle Charlie asked. "Nothing short of near-death itself would keep him away from these Christmas parties. He's been playing Santa for—how many years is it, Mr. Jenkins?"

"No matter now, Charlie. No matter. We've got to find another Santa and quick!"

A Bright Idea

"Well, Mr. Jenkins, you could . . ." Uncle Charlie began.

"Me!" Mr. Jenkins threw his despairing hands out in a gesture that made Charlie and his nephew realize that Mr. Jenkins could not have weighed more than 130 pounds.

"But, Charlie, you—yes indeed. You could play Santa Claus," Mr. Jenkins exulted.

"But I . . ."

"No buts about it. Here let's hustle you off. The children are waiting." In seconds the white jacketed maître d'hôtel was transformed into a brilliant red Santa.

John Thomas couldn't believe his eyes. A colored Santa Claus—and in this exclusive club! His chest began to swell pridefully.

The Mask

Mr. Jenkins was delighted. He made appreciative little clucking sounds as he adjusted the belt. "And your nephew can be Santa's helper," Mr. Jenkins said expansively.

"Oh yes, Charlie, here's your mask." He handed Uncle Charlie the pasty white mask from which streamed a snowy yak-hair beard.

John Thomas lowered his eyes. Uncle Charlie wasn't going to be a colored Santa Claus. He was going to pass for a white Santa.

Charlie saw the change of expression in his nephew's eyes. He held the mask in his hands as Mr. Jenkins pushed him through the door.

"I'll call you in a minute, John Thomas," he said, lifting the mask to his face. "You're going to help me, you know."

John Thomas didn't answer. Suddenly the ache in his body was too heavy to bear. If there couldn't even be a colored Santa Claus, then there couldn't be a colored mayor or president, or a colored police chief or four-star general.

Tears brimmed in his eyes and he fought manfully to keep them from spilling down his tight little cheek.

Loving Santa

The muffled shouts of the joyous children came through to him. "Santa! Santa! We love you Santa!" They loved Santa all right—but not Uncle Charlie who was underneath—passing.

Suddenly someone burst through the door. It was one of the youngsters John Thomas remembered from other parties. His eyes were shining bright.

"Your uncle says to come on. We're going to help pass out the presents and some of the other kids are going to pass the food out. Chef's sick, you know. Say, your Uncle Charlie sure makes a keen Santa Claus."

How did he know it was Uncle Charlie? The boy pulled John Thomas to his feet and toward the gala Assembly Room. There before a tree that towered almost to the ceiling stood Uncle Charlie.

He was dressed as Santa Claus all right, but there was no mask over his beaming brown face. The young children clung to his legs and pulled at him.

What had happened? Then he heard his uncle's voice. "There are my helpers. Come on boys, the presents are high and the children are waiting," and John Thomas was swept into the holiday mood.

The Party Ends

Finally the party was over. The last present had been opened, the last marshmallow in the last cup of cocoa had been captured. The children were gone home.

John Thomas stood close to his uncle. What would they do to him for going out there like that—without the mask?

What would the club men think of the colored Santa Claus? Maybe they'd even fire Uncle Charlie. The boy would not have his uncle's side, a fierce new pride burned in him.

There was Mr. Jenkins coming. Uncle Charlie was packing away the Santa suit.

Mr. Jenkins was solemn. He held out his hand to Uncle Charlie. "Nice job, Charlie, nice job. That was a pretty fine speech you made about Santa Claus representing the brotherhood of man and the love for little children."

The Best Thing

"Taking that mask off was the best thing you could have done. You made the children understand what Christmas really is."

His voice was warm and a little tremulous around the edges. He looked straight into Uncle Charlie's eyes and he went on quietly "You've got me believing in Santa Claus again myself."

The two men shook hands and Mr. Jenkins turned to John Thomas. "Your uncle's already gotten his Christmas bonus from the club and I know he wouldn't take this money for being Santa Claus so I'm going to give it to you, John Thomas.

"Save it for your college education, son. Your uncle's told me how he's saving to help send you through. God bless you both, merry Christmas!"

He pressed the crisp bills into the boy's hands and was gone. The kitchen was strangely silent. Uncle Charlie wrapped a few sandwiches up. "We're to take some home to Mama?" the boy nodded eagerly.

A few hours ago he wouldn't have been caught dead taking a thing home from this kitchen. Now he wanted to share as much of this magic afternoon with his mother as he could.

White Christmas Approaches

The two shrugged into their coats and Uncle Charlie closed the outside door behind him, making sure the kitchen area was locked up. A moist snow flake brushed John Thomas's warm cheek. He held out his hand to catch a few.

"Looks like we're going to have a white Christmas," he said, making small talk and falling in with his uncle's long stride.

"Is that good or bad, John Thomas?"

John Thomas smiled because he knew his uncle was not asking about the weather. "I guess it depends on how you look at it, huh Uncle Charlie."

Uncle Charlie got his hand on the boy's shoulder as the pair trudged out of the driveway. A great weight was lifted from the man because he knew now that John Thomas understood many, many things.

He had given the boy back his self-respect, a present that would grow with the youngster for all the Christmases to come.

SOURCES

MARGARET BLACK "A Christmas Party That Prevented a Split in the Church," *Baltimore Afro-American*, December 23, 1916.

JOHN HENRIK CLARKE "Santa Claus Is a White Man," *Opportunity*, December 1939.

FANNY JACKSON COPPIN "Christmas Eve Story," *A.M.E. Christian Recorder*, December 23, 1880.

ANDREW DOBSON "The Devil Spends Christmas Eve in Dixie," *Chicago Defender*, December 22, 1934.

W. E. B. DU BOIS "The Sermon in the Cradle," *Crisis*, December 1921.

ALICE MOORE DUNBAR "The Children's Christmas," *Indianapolis Freeman*, December 25, 1897.

TIMOTHY THOMAS FORTUNE "Mirama's Christmas Test," *Indianapolis Freeman*, December 19, 1896.

ADELE HAMLIN "Merry Christmas Eve," *Baltimore Afro-American*, December 25, 1948.

AUGUSTUS M. HODGES "The Christmas Reunion Down at Martinsville," *Indianapolis Freeman*, December 29, 1894.

"Three Men and a Woman," *Indianapolis Freeman*, December 20 and 27, 1902; January 3, 10, 17, and 31; May 30, June 6, and July 4 and 11, 1903.

PAULINE ELIZABETH HOPKINS "General Washington: A Christmas Story," *Colored American Magazine*, December 1900.

LANGSTON HUGHES "One Christmas Eve," *Opportunity*, December 1933.

JAMES CONWAY JACKSON "Uncle U.S. Santa Claus," *Washington Bee*, December 27, 1913.

MARY JENNESS "A Carol of Color," *Opportunity*, December 1927.

MARY E. LEE "Mollie's Best Christmas Gift," *Christian Recorder*, December 31, 1885.

LELIA PLUMMER "The Autobiography of a Dollar Bill," *Colored American Magazine*, December 1904.

LOUIS LORENZO REDDING "A Christmas Journey," *Opportunity*, December, 1925.

BRUCE L. REYNOLDS "It Came to Pass: A Christmas Story," *Chicago Defender*, December 23, 1939.

CARRIE JANE THOMAS "A Christmas Story," *Christian Recorder*, December 24, 1885.

KATHERINE DAVIS TILLMAN "Fannie May's Christmas," *Christian Recorder*, December 29, 1921.

SALEM TUTT WHITNEY "Elsie's Christmas," *Indianapolis Freeman*, December 28, 1912.

VALENA MINOR WILLIAMS "White Christmas," *Baltimore Afro-American*, December 19, 1953.